Gabriel's Watch

Year of publication 2014 by Devil's Highway
First printed in 2008

www.devilshighway.net

Cover design by Clarissa Yeo
www.yocladesigns.com

ISBN: 978-0-9930500-0-8

GABRIEL'S WATCH

CROSSGRAVE: BOOK ONE

Sandra D. Sims

For Kris

1.
Karen

The children ran through the trees and down the hill, laughing and playing as they did almost every day. Autumn was always the best time of year to play on The Watch. Fallen leaves crunched beneath their feet as they raced; the four children slid down the slippery slope of the hill and scrambled back up again. Looking up towards the bare treetops, the long branches twirled about the glaring sun, the rays shone through the yellow-brown leaves making dappled patterns on the children's little faces.

As their laughter echoed and bounced around the trees, some startled crows took flight from their perch. The children followed them, running down the hill again. Once they gathered speed it was always hard to stop, they laughed all the way down and half-screamed whenever the ground became too slippery. As she neared the bottom of the hill, Karen lost her footing and tripped, she stumbled through the edge of the woods and into the road. She picked herself up, but too late. Her screams merged with the sound of skidding tyres.

2.
Kevin

2001

Kevin Marshall woke with a start; his dream interrupted by his alarm. He sat up, groaning. Every night he dreamed about his sister and, for the split second upon awaking, he would feel relief that it was just a dream. Then he would remember that it was real: she was gone. Even after all these years he still felt responsible for Karen's death. He remembered seeing her lying there, in the road. Was there something he could have done to stop it? He could think of nothing that he could have done differently, yet the though still plagued him.

It had been eight years since it happened.

Realising that his alarm was still beeping at him, attempting to bring him back to the real world, Kevin picked up the clock and lobbed it across the room. From downstairs, his mother called out to him.

"Yes, I'm up!" he shouted back. He swung his legs out of bed, rested his feet on the floor and sat staring at them for a few moments while gathering his thoughts. Standing up and pulling on his khaki cargo pants, he scanned his bedroom floor for a relatively clean T-shirt; finding one, he pulled it over his head.

His mobile rang. Looking at the screen, Kevin saw that it was Peter calling. He answered it. “All right, Pete?” He sat back down on the bed and pulled on a pair of scruffy old trainers. Peter wanted to confirm that they were meeting later – they had had quite a bit to drink the night before, celebrating their friend's birthday, and any plans they had made were a little hazy. Kevin had not forgotten.

“You bringing some gear?” Peter asked.

“As always.” Kevin smiled, already rummaging through his bottom draw to recover his hidden stash of tobacco, Rizlas, and a bag of marijuana – one of the perks of the job he did for Sean Reilly. He shoved the items into his pockets. “I'll see you around midday,” he added. “I've got to see Sean this morning.” On the other end of the telephone, he heard Peter groan. “He's not that bad,” Kevin said defensively.

“He is,” Peter replied.

Ending the call and shoving his mobile into his pocket, Kevin made his way downstairs. He was looking forward to an afternoon on The Watch, but first he had business to attend to. He walked through to the kitchen, where his mother, Amanda, sat at the table, feeding his baby sister, Maisie.

"What do you want for breakfast, Ke...?"

"Can't stop, mum," he said, cutting her off and giving her a kiss on the cheek, "busy."

"Kevin, you have to eat!" she called after him as he slipped out through the back door and disappeared for the day. Amanda huffed. "Your brother will be the death of me," she said, turning to Maisie, who looked up innocently from her high-chair.

Walking down the road towards the high street, Kevin took one of the bands from around his wrist and tied back his shoulder-length, brown hair. He always kept hair bands with him in case he lost or broke one. Long hair was a nuisance; he had toyed with the idea of shaving it off, but could not bring himself to do it.

Reaching the end of the road, Kevin paused for a moment and stared up at the imposing hill in the distance. He would be scaling its slopes later, but first he had things to do. Kevin lit a cigarette; turned and walked along the high street.

3.
Bethany

In her tiny closet of a room, Bethany Matthews slept, spread out on her stomach across her bed. System of a Down were playing on her stereo; she had put that CD on loop when she staggered in the night before. She always left her music on; it gave her a sense of comfort as well as drowning out the noise her uncle made as he stumbled home drunk late at night.

On one side of her room cluttered shelves filled the entire wall, making the room appear so much smaller. The few clothes she had were strewn across the floor. The blind at the window was closed - sunlight never saw this room, neither did a vacuum cleaner. Not that Bethany cared; she was rarely at home any more. She preferred to stay out all night if she could; only going home to eat or sleep if she had nowhere else to go.

'Toxicity' was playing for the umpteenth time as Bethany slowly started to regain consciousness. Her telephone was ringing. Like a separate organism, her arm reached up to the shelf at the head of her bed and searched for the receiver. Finding it, she slowly raised her head and answered. “Nngh...ugh..Hello?”

“Good morning, Beth!” said the voice on the other end, it was Peter. “How's the hangover?”

“Ugh!” she replied. “I hate morning people!”

“You're coming to The Watch later,” Peter told her. “No arguments.”

Bethany checked the time on the little alarm clock; it was quarter past ten, she could not believe that Peter was calling her at such an ungodly hour, nor could she stand how unbelievably chirpy he was following last night's drinking binge. Then again, the guy had a special talent for drinking twice as much as anyone else and not even slurring his speech.

“The Watch? Cool,” Bethany murmured, beginning to feel more awake. “I just have to make myself presentable, then I'll be there.”

“Okay,” Peter chuckled, “see you in about four hours then!”

“Hey!” said an already disgruntled Bethany. “You'll regret that!”

4.
The Watch

1992

It was the first time her brother had taken her up to the top of The Watch. Karen had seen the beauty of it from her bedroom window and had walked on the green at the foot of the hill, but the apex was a magical, mysterious place where she dreamed of going. Her parents were wary of letting her out, but her big brother Kevin promised to look after her. Now, they were ascending to the very top of The Watch, a place where he would often visit with their friends.

They walked further up the hill then through the small woods. As they reached the other side of the trees, they came to a stone staircase with iron railings running along it. To one side of the railings were thick, unkempt shrubs and more trees. On the other there were a few scattered trees and amongst them hid worn headstones, covered with ivy – lost monuments to those long dead and long since forgotten.

Hand in hand, Kevin and Karen climbed the staircase, it was steep and went on forever, in Karen's mind. Finally, they reached the top. It was breath-taking. A beautiful stone statue of an angel, stretching high above the hill, dominated the landscape before the old church. The latter was unremarkable, other than to say that it was falling down, dangerous and their parents had warned them not to play there. A path extended from the church to an opening where iron gates would have once stood; iron fences flanked either side of the path, separating it from further headstones.

The tall, stone statue towered above a small promenade; from here the whole North side of the town could be seen - giving the hill its name, The Watch. On the south side of the hill, there was a private school and several opulent houses – an impressive sight, but nothing compared to what the decaying churchyard had to offer.

The large statue, facing North and looking down on the town, was said to be a representation of the Archangel Gabriel. Her folded wings reaching nearly nine feet and her right arm stretched outwards and upwards towards the heavens while her left arm held something close to her chest, though no one knew what that was as it had broken off about a hundred years before.

Gabriel, the Archangel of mercy and retribution, looked on over the people of her town, the aptly named Gabriel's Watch.

The statue was prominent enough to be seen clearly from the town, an imposing source of inspiration to many. At over four-hundred and fifty feet, The Watch was the highest point for miles around.

Kevin and Peter walked along the outskirts of St Michael's CofE Primary School. Tall iron railings sat atop a four foot wall, stretching around the perimeter. The boys remembered attending the school when they were children, it still looked – and felt – like a prison. Just outside the school gates was an old, red telephone box and leaning against it was Bethany, staring off into the distance. She was a tall, skinny girl who seldom smiled, she had both hands in the pockets of her cut-off denim shorts and a flimsy, green mesh top hung off her boyish frame. Her short, bobbed hair had been dyed a dark red and matched her ox-blood Dr. Marten boots. Her left arm was overloaded with wristbands; the right simply bore a watch.

She nodded her head in time to the music playing on her personal stereo. Then, suddenly aware that she had company, Bethany whipped off her headphones, treating her friends to a tinny dose of Nirvana.

Peter grinned at her. "Nice of you to join us."

"Well, I couldn't let you guys go on without me, could I?" she replied. Kevin smiled as he stood with his hands in his pockets, he nodded towards the hill.

"Shall we head up to The Watch, then?"

"No, dude," Bethany replied. "I was planning on leaning against this 'phone box all day!" As she walked ahead of the two boys, Kevin informed her that sarcasm was the lowest form of wit. Bethany waved him off dismissively as they set upon the long walk leading up to the top of The Watch.

Sitting on one of the benches that stretched along the promenade, Bethany gazed out over the town. Kevin, who was cross-legged on the ground with his back to a stone balustrade, finished rolling a joint and handed it to her. "Happy birthday, Beth," he said. "Everything's legal from today!" As Bethany lit the spliff, Kevin added: "well, almost everything.

"That just makes everything less fun, doesn't it?" She pouted mockingly before taking her first drag. "Anyway," she added, "didn't we celebrate my birthday yesterday? Not that I remember any of it."

While it was true they had marked the occasion already, Bethany's birthday was a milestone and her friends intended to make it memorable.

"We're celebrating again for good measure," said Peter. "It's not every day that one turns eighteen."

Bethany took another drag from the roll-up as she regarded him for a few seconds. Peter, who was of West Indian descent, was always well turned out and anything other than shirts and trousers looked ridiculous on him, he did own some T-shirts but most of them had been pilfered by Bethany. He also had an accent that betrayed his well-to-do upbringing.

"You're really quite posh, aren't you, Pete?" she said as she handed him the joint. Kevin sniggered, and seeing the two figures moving towards them along the promenade, he said: "Oh, look. We've got company."

5.
Friends

Alex and Natalie, a couple from their circle of acquaintances, strolled along the path. Kevin always said that those two could smell a joint from three miles away. They were tolerated simply because it was better to have them on side than not. Life was hard enough without making enemies.

Natalie was a voluptuous woman with shoulder-length, blonde hair, although for some reason, she saw fit to bleach it even blonder. She wore a short, black dress, which was much too tight for her and made her bulge. She waddled along in ankle boots with heels that made it difficult to walk. Natalie's arm encircled Alex's waist; he was a little taller than her and his arm curled around her shoulders. He was dressed all in black with large key-chains hanging from the pockets of his cargo pants. It was the same attire they had been wearing the night before and they reeked of alcohol; they had been out all night – and all morning.

"All right, dudes?" Alex offered the group a friendly smile and focusing his attention on Bethany, he added: "How's the birthday girl?"

"Hungover," she replied, the smell of booze on his breath making her feel worse. Natalie stood by Alex's side and smiled unconvincingly at the group, who nodded in acknowledgement of her being there. Natalie did not particularly like anybody, which was just as well, because nobody liked her either.

Alex sat cross-legged on the ground beside Kevin, and Natalie dutifully followed suit. "So, how's it going?" he asked. Everyone responded in the usual, vague manner; work was okay, college was okay, everything was fine. The group did not mind talking to Alex because, although they thought of him as idiotic at times, he was at least friendly; unlike Natalie, who sat there, scowling.

Kevin was still waiting for that all-important question that Alex always asked him.

"So, Marshall," he said. "What have we got on offer today?" There it was. Every time without fail the conversation would swiftly turn to what was on offer. It was the only reason why these two groups ever interacted with each other. Kevin often felt like a hypocrite; with the exception of marijuana, he never tried what he sold. He never would try anything else and neither would his friends, but selling was easy money and Alex and Natalie were two of his best customers.

They would smoke anything and Natalie had recently tempted Alex into trying heroin, thought he would usually just take what was going at the time. He was not dependant on the drug, but Natalie was beginning to feel that she could not function without it. She was developing the look of an addict; losing weight and getting dark rings around her eyes, which were carelessly covered with dark make-up.

"I'm not selling today," said Kevin. "I'm purely socialising."

"Hey, that's cool," Alex replied. It probably was. They most likely already had some of what they wanted, they just wanted more of it. If they did not get it from Kevin they could find it somewhere else, and quickly at that.

They did not stay long, they rarely did, disappearing into the churchyard. The others were relieved to be left alone in their little clique again.

"Thank fuck for that!" Peter said, when they were finally out of earshot.

"Yeah," Bethany agreed. "She's probably gone to suck her boyfriend's cock in a dark corner somewhere!"

The boys turned to stare at her , silently

aghast.

"What?!" she exclaimed. Bethany had often stated that girls like Natalie gave the rest of their gender a bad name. Kevin laughed out loud. "Miaow!" he said. Peter, laughed and nodded in agreement.

"You're getting rather bitchy in your old age!"

"Why, thank you," she said, sitting up proudly and grinning widely.

Peter nudged her. "You're not going to make many friends saying things like that, you know."

"True," Bethany replied. "And with you two deserting me to go to uni at the end of the year, I'm going to need all the friends I can get!"

Bethany did not go to college like the two boys; she worked in the record shop on the high street, a job which suited her just fine, as she loved music. Kevin was quite the artist, he saw himself in a career in graphics or web-site design. As for Peter, he spent a long time deciding whether to be a lawyer, like his mother or a doctor, like his father. In the end he chose neither, deciding to use his talents as a pianist to teach music.

"We'll still keep in touch, Beth," Peter said.

"You might not want to," she replied,

“once you're hanging out with your posh, intellectual friends at Cambridge.”

“Who said I was going to Ca-?”

“Oh, come on, Beth!” Kevin interrupted. “Where else are we going to get our daily fix of sarcasm?”

“And there I was, thinking that sarcasm was the lowest form of wit.”

Kevin did not have much to say in response.

“Anyway,” Peter laughed. “We're not going too far away, so we can keep an eye on you.” He put his arm around Bethany's shoulder and she patted him on the hand.

“Thanks,” she replied, “but I can look after myself, you know.”

“It's not you we're worried about!” Kevin scoffed. Bethany laughed mockingly and flicked a 'V' sign at him. She was well known for being abrasive, sometimes even insensitive, but that was only on the surface. Underneath there was a strength and honesty that people admired, so they forgave her her bluntness.

Despite Bethany's apparent ferocity and their constant ribbing of each other, the three of them had looked out for each other since the day they met. None of them relished the fact that they would be separated at the end of the year, when the boys would go to university.

The afternoon seemed to have passed by all too quickly. Leaning on the stone balustrade, they looked over the town.

"What shall we do tonight, guys?" Kevin asked. They pondered for a moment, as nice as it was up there, they could not stay on The Watch all night.

"Pub?" Bethany suggested. Before either of the boys could answer, they heard an awful cry from within the churchyard. Startled, they stared at each other silently. Then came another scream.

Bethany was the first to act; she ran towards the sound of the screams. Peter and Kevin were close behind her. Pushing her way through the overgrown vegetation, Bethany found them and stopped dead in her tracks.

"Shit," she whispered. The boys came to a halt just behind her and stared in shock. Peter turned away and resisted the urge to vomit. Through her howling, Natalie finally looked up at them. "I can't wake him up!" she sobbed. She was kneeling over Alex, her head resting on his chest while he lay there motionless, his skin pale and blue around the lips.

"Fuck!" Kevin grabbed his mobile and dialled 999.

Everything was a blur. Alex's body had been zipped into a bag and carted away. In the street, where an ambulance and several police cars were parked, a crowd had gathered to peer through the railings to watch the commotion. Natalie sat on the ground with her knees pulled up to her chest and her arms curled tightly around them. Silently rocking back and forth, she stared into space. A police officer had taken the rest of the group aside and started to ask questions.

"Were you friends with the deceased and his girlfriend?"

"Not really, we were acquaintances." *But only when it suited them.*

"Do you know what they were taking?"

"No." *But we can take a wild guess.*

"Are you in possession of any drugs?"

"No." *We smoked it all.*

They each gave their account of what happened, with the exception of Natalie, who was making no sense at all.

"What's going to happen to her?" Bethany

asked one of the officers.

"We'll take her down to the station," he said, "and let her sleep it off until she's ready to give a statement."

"She's not going to be in any trouble, is she?"

The officer gave her a solemn look. "Don't worry," he said. "Your friend's going to be all right." He made an attempt to smile and squeezed Bethany on the shoulder before walking over to his colleague.

"Thanks." She crossed her arms and scowled. *That didn't really answer my question.*

One of the officers tried to help Natalie up from the ground.

"Get off!" she yelled, flailing her arms. She was unwilling to be moved from the spot, but a second officer came to the aid of the first and they each took hold of an arm. Natalie, now kicking and screaming was dragged to a marked police car.

"No! Get away from me!" she screamed. "I have to wait for him! I have to stay here 'til Alex gets back!" Once inside the back of the car her screams could still be heard, though slightly muffled. "He said he'd be back soon!" Natalie pounded at the window with her fists. "He said he'd be back!"

The group stared in silence at Natalie's display, whether it was the shock or the effects of something she had smoked, they could not tell. Only half aware that someone was speaking to them, they turned their attention back to the police officer who had questioned them a few moments ago. They stared blankly and the man had to repeat himself.

“We'll need the three of you to come down to the station sometime tomorrow to make an official statement,” he said. Turning to Bethany, he added: “And I know you're worried about your friend...”

“Just look after her, okay?” She promptly turned and walked back towards the promenade, closely followed by Peter. Kevin looked at the officer, shrugged, then left in pursuit of his friends.

He found the pair of them leaning against the balcony that overlooked the town. Bethany looked pale, more so than usual. “You okay?” he asked. After a while, Bethany finally looked up and shrugged.

“Do you think she'll be all right?” she said.

“I'm sure she'll be fine,” Peter replied, squeezing her shoulder. “Besides, when did you start giving a toss about Natalie?”

“I don't, really,” Bethany shrugged, “but

that's not the point, is it?" She sighed heavily and stared back into the churchyard. "I wouldn't wish that on anyone," she continued. "I just feel bad, you know, for all those times I was a bitch and took the piss out of the pair of them."

Peter put his arm around Bethany as her tears started to flow.

"Hey, come on," he said, "it's not your fault, you weren't to know."

"They're a pair of losers," Kevin said, "if you mess around with the kind of shit that they do, something like this is bound to happen."

Bethany's sobbing quickly subsided. "Even so, no one deserves that."

"I see your point." Kevin agreed, looking over his shoulder through the churchyard, he could make out a few people still loitering near the gates at the other side. "Especially with that group of twats who have turned up just to have a good look."

"Morbid bastards," Muttered Peter. Bethany let out a little laugh.

"I think she's going to be all right!" Kevin said as he hugged her.

The sky was starting to grow dark; where had the day gone? They toyed with the idea of going in search of food, but the thought of eating anything made them feel queasy.

"I think I just want to go home." Bethany sighed. "I'm tired."

"Come back to my place," said Peter. "I don't think you should be on your own." Bethany just shrugged, and then nodded in resigned agreement. Peter looked at Kevin, who appeared to be distracted. "Are you coming with us, Marshall?" he asked.

"No, you two go on," he replied. "I want to be on my own for a while."

"Well, you know where to find us," Peter said as he and Bethany started the walk back towards town.

Watching them as they disappeared along the promenade, Kevin made himself comfortable on one of the benches, happy to have his own company and to reflect on his thoughts. He considered the fact that he could be partly responsible for what happened to Alex. Had Kevin sold him something that gave him the final nudge over the edge? Was the stuff he sold bad? How could he know if he never tried it? Kevin was not sure of anything, at this point he did not want to know. The only thing he was sure of, was that he wanted to give up selling, he was just unsure of how to go about it.

"It's terrible, what happened, isn't it?" he

heard a voice say. Kevin looked up sharply, vexed at the interruption. His irritation faded as soon as he saw her. Not only was he too polite to tell her to go away, he found that he did not mind the interruption when he saw that she was beautiful, very beautiful. She was fair-haired and porcelain skinned with celestial blue eyes. Dressed in pale, flowing colours, she looked like an angel. The girl seemed familiar to Kevin, but he could not quite place where he had seen her before.

"Was he a friend of yours?" the girl asked.

"Not really," Kevin replied, smiling to himself, "more of a colleague."

"It's okay, if you'd rather be alone..." she said, perhaps sensing his initial agitation.

"Don't be silly," said Kevin, as he made space for her on the bench. "Sit down."

"I'm new to the area," the girl continued. "I was told this place would be worth checking out." She sighed and shook her head. "Although, I don't think this is quite what I had in mind!"

"Yeah, you're telling me." Kevin lit a cigarette and offered one to the girl.

"Oh, I don't smoke," she said. "It's bad for you."

"Yeah, you're probably right." Kevin let out a bitter laugh as he exhaled. He extended and arm to shake the girl's hand. “My friends call me Marshall.”

“Pleased to meet you, Marshall.” She smiled, accepting the open hand, “My name's Karen.”

6.
Remember, Remember

1993

There were some who said The Watch was haunted, Kevin believed that. There were many myths surrounding that mysterious hill, and numerous tales told of strange happenings and eerie encounters. Some said that the church bell could be heard ringing at midnight, although it was said that the church tower was missing its bell and the clock ceased working decades ago. There were those who believed that the hill was an ancient burial ground for a race of noble warriors.

There were countless stories of sightings and supernatural events; lonely spirits trying to settle old scores or watch over loved ones, but there was one rumour in particular that intrigued Kevin.

Along the foot of the hill, motorists had described sightings of a girl. She would appear in front of them, as if from nowhere; sometimes she would be running across the road, and other times standing perfectly still. Each time the account was slightly different, the girl's looks would always change; different hair, different clothes, a different age every time. Three things, however, stayed exactly the same in every case; the girl's eyes would stare fixedly on the driver, the driver would hit the girl and, every time, they would step out of the car to help the injured girl, only to discover that she had vanished.

The Marshalls buried Karen on her birthday, the fifth of November, Bonfire Night. A tiny child in a tiny box, she looked as though she was just asleep. Kevin stood by her coffin, silently begging her to wake up, not to leave him alone in this world. He barely spoke for months following his sister's death. For a long time he avoided The Watch, where the accident happened. Even as he grew older, Kevin avoided the South side of the hill, facing North he could deal with, but the actual spot where his little sister lost her life brought back too many haunting memories. Passing by in the car, Kevin would turn his face away; he could never see that part of the hill without feeling sick. It reminded him of Karen sleeping peacefully in her little white box. It was so unfair, she was not even nine years old.

He remembered how his father had squeezed his shoulder as he stared at the coffin. "Be brave, young Marshall," he said. "Your mother needs us to be strong." Soon after that, his father left and Kevin did not see him for five years.

Peter entered his flat with Bethany in tow. The place had been left to him by his mother; it still felt strange and quiet, not having her around. She had died the year before and her absence was felt just as keenly now as it was back then. His uncle had stayed with him for a few months after the funeral, and once satisfied that Peter was ready to cope on his own, he returned to Trinidad. Bethany had been there on an almost daily basis – making a nuisance of herself, as she would put it – but Peter was glad of her presence, at least that part of his life continued as normal.

He and his mother had moved into this flat from the suburbs after his father's fall from grace; they were not rich any more, but they were not poor either. Not that Peter cared about that, he only wished his family had not been torn apart. His inheritance, together with his part-time job meant that he could live quite comfortably and continue his studies. Things could have been a lot worse, so Peter tried to focus on the positives rather than his family's misfortunes.

Heading straight for the fridge, Bethany yanked the door open and eyed up the contents. She had stayed there so many times that courtesy was no longer a necessity, she treated the place like it was her own, and Peter would not have it any other way. Finding some orange juice, Bethany was about to drink from the carton when Peter scolded her. She tutted, rolled her eyes at his and fetched a glass from the cupboard. After pouring the juice and returning the carton to the fridge, Bethany mockingly raised her glass to Peter. Then she remembered her manners.

"Oh, sorry, did you want one?"

"No, thanks." Peter shook his head and laughed. "I'll make us something to eat."

From the bathroom, Peter could hear the sound of dishes clattering in the kitchen. That was one of the great thing about Bethany, she was always very tidy, especially in other people's houses. Leaning against the sink, Peter stared at his reflection in the mirror. Though they had never been close, he felt pangs of empathy for Natalie. Losing a loved one was bad enough, but being the one to find them...

Peter let out a heavy sigh, nausea creeping through him. He tried not to think about it, but trying only made him think of it more. He continued to stare blankly into the mirror until his trance was broken by a knock on the door.

“I'm borrowing a T-shirt,” came Bethany's voice.

“Okay,” Peter replied. He would have no T-shirts left at this rate. They were both tall and slim so his things fit her, and even though they were a little baggy, his T-shirts looked better on Bethany than they did on him.

Realising he had left the tap running, Peter splashed some cold water to his face and as he did so, he heard a voice in his head: *She's about to find out*. Did he imagine that? Catching a glimpse of a face in the mirror, Peter spun around; no one there. He swung back to the mirror where he saw no face but his own. *She's about to find out*? What could that possibly mean? Peter frowned, he had seen that face before, almost every day, in fact, but never quite so clearly.

Turning the tap off, Peter took a few deep breaths in an attempt to compose himself, he opened the door and made his way down the hall. Passing his bedroom, he stopped as he saw Bethany standing there. She was facing away from him but he could tell she was tense, her back arched as her hands leaned on the chest of drawers. Her head bowed, staring into the drawer which lay open. Surely he could not have been stupid enough to hide it there? Why was she going through his things? Then he remembered the T-shirt.

"Beth?" he asked, hoping that she had not just found what he thought she had, that there was something else the matter.

"Pete..." Bethany's voice quivered as she turned to face him. "Why do you have a gun?"

7.
Peter

Peter Crossgrave sat and waited. *They always keep you waiting in this place,* he thought. He pondered all the questions that swam around his head, he needed to see his father, yet he dreaded the visit. Eventually, he was allowed to go through, Peter had not seen his father for some weeks and was glad that he was there now; and his father, as always, was pleased to see him.

"Dad!" Sorry it's been so long." The two men hugged each other, and from a few feet away, a warden gave them a disapproving look.

"Oh, I forgot," said Peter, "you're not allowed to hug in these places."

"Just ignore him, son," his father replied. "All wardens are miserable, it's in the job description." They sniggered and the warden, aware that they were talking about him, turned and walked away to cast his glances elsewhere. The two of them sat down at a table.

Peter's father, Dr. Philip Crossgrave, was a friendly, cheerful looking man. He wore glasses and had large, puffy cheeks that resembled a hamster. Philip was, more often than not, an approachable man, but Peter was apprehensive about talking to him today.

"It's good to see you, son," Philip said. Peter only smiled and stayed silent, his father knew that something was wrong. "How is everything?" he asked, hoping that his son would tell him rather than making him guess.

Peter bowed his head. "Bad," was all he said.

Philip sighed as he realised that he would have to prod further to get anything out of him. Sometimes, talking to his son was like trying to prise limpets off a rock.

"You're not having trouble getting into university are you?" he asked. "Or problems at work?"

"No, college is fine." Peter sighed, staring down at the table. "It's nothing to do with that."

"Then what's the problem?" his father persisted.

Peter's voice was low and flat. "You know my friend, Bethany..."

"Ah, I see," Philip grinned. "Trouble in Paradise?"

"No, Dad." Peter shook his head, and for the first time, looked up to meet his father's gaze. The smiled faded from Philip's lips, he could tell that whatever was bothering Peter was serious.

"You'd better spit it out, son." He sat back and folded his arms, watching Peter and waiting.

Unable to think of anything to say, Peter stared dumbly, just like he had when Bethany had confronted him. His silence had been more damaging than the truth, he had let her walk away, did not try to explain. He had seen her scared before, but never that frightened, and never of him. That disturbed him.

Now he had to think of a way to explain that to his father. Letting out a deep breath, Peter began again. "It's Bethany," his voice gained a slight quiver. "um... she found that gun." Peter cleared his throat as his eyes left his father's gaze again.

"What?" Philip's voice was somewhere between a less and a whisper. He leaned over the table towards Peter, desperately trying to keep his voice down. "Have you still got that thing? What the hell is wrong with you?!"

"I'm sorry..." Peter said feebly.

"Sorry?" his father spat. "Do you have any idea how much shit we're going to be in if she goes to the police?"

Peter leaned forward, mirroring his father.

"No one's going to find out," he said. "Beth wouldn't tell anyone, I know that."

"You're sure of that, are you?" Philip said, making sure his son looked him in the eye when he answered.

Peter nodded. "I trust her."

Philip sighed; he hoped his son was right. He continued to stare at Peter, he was not finished with him yet.

"Why didn't you get rid of the damn thing when I told you to?" he hissed. Peter rested his elbow on the table with his head cupped in his hand. He could sense his father was glaring at him, but he looked away, avoiding his eyes.

Peter shrugged and answered his question. "I wasn't thinking," he said.

"You never do, that's your problem." Philip's composure was much calmer now; he was trying not to be too harsh with his son. He clasped his hands in front of him and tried to keep his tone even. "You'd better get rid of that thing as soon as possible," he said, "before it causes any more damage. And really get rid of it this time, no hiding it. Being your father won't stop me from kicking your arse."

"How are you going to kick my arse from behind bars?" Peter retorted, meeting his father's disapproving gaze head on. He cleared his throat and looked away. “Sorry.” Looking up again he added: “You shouldn't be in here.”

“No one should be in here,” Philip smiled and looked around him. “Didn't you know, son? Everyone in here is innocent!”

Peter let out a laugh. The tension between them dissipated, but Peter still felt a slight pang of pain. “Seriously,” he said, “you shouldn't be in here.”

Philip sighed and leaned closer to his son. “Peter, what I did was best for everyone,” he said. “You do know that, don't you?”

As he looked into his father's eyes, a tear rolled down Peter's cheek.

“I've screwed up,” he whispered.

“Now, look here,” Philip's voice sounded sterner than he had meant it to. “I won't hear you talk like that. We've all made mistakes,” he went on, “I have nothing but respect for the man that you've become. I'm proud of you and I know your mother would be too.” Philip watched his son closely, Peter stared silently back at him. “I would happily stay here for all eternity,” Philip continued, “knowing that your mother was still around to look after you. You could have been on your own a lot sooner. I have no regrets because I can see you work hard to keep your life together."

Peter looked down and fiddled with the cuff of his shirt. Philip hated seeing him so dispirited, he looked around again, to make sure none of the guards were within earshot.

"Think about it," he said. "if things had happened differently we would all be in our graves now; you, me and your mother."

Peter did not take much consolation in this, but he saw the logic. He just nodded his agreement.

Trying to lighten the mood, Philip patted his son on the hand. "Come on, tell me what else is going on," he said. "We rarely get to see each other, give me some happy news."

Peter shrugged, there was not much to tell; he was working hard and waiting for interviews at university. Philip asked after Peter's friends and he responded that they were all fine. They sat in silence for a few moments before Philip spoke again.

"You know son, we do have television and newspapers in here. I heard about that boy that died, Alex? Did you know him?" Peter nodded. Philip leaned across the table. "Do you want to talk about it?"

Peter looked at him and considered it for a moment, then thought better of it.

"Not really," he said, shrugging, then shaking his head.

"How's his girlfriend holding up?" Philip asked as though he had not heard Peter's reply.

"Natalie?" Peter shrugged. "She's disappeared; no one's seen her for a while."

"That's too bad," Philip said, more to himself than to his son. Seeing that his father was on the verge of asking more questions, Peter stopped him.

"Dad, can we please talk about something else?"

"What do you want to talk about?" Philip asked.

"Well," Peter started to fidget, "it's just... I miss her." Philip tried to think of something to say that could make Peter's mood a happier one, and seeing that this was probably the wrong time to try, father took son by the hand.

"I know, Peter," he said. "I miss your mother too."

8.
Thick as Thieves

Peter slumped into one of the armchairs in the living room. He always felt a little down after visiting his father, but today somehow seemed worse. He was used to having someone there to talk to, and since his mother's death, that someone had been Bethany. Plucking his mobile from his pocket, Peter dialled her number. There was no answer – again. Perhaps she intended to avoid him for ever.

Heaving a sigh, Peter went into his bedroom and retrieved the gun – the source of all his trouble - which was now wedged firmly underneath his mattress. *How the hell do you get rid of one of these things anyway*? He thought. That was a good point. How did one dispose of a weapon? Peter shoved the gun back under his bed, he would deal with it later, and right now he had more important things to sort out.

Getting up, Peter caught a glimpse of a familiar face in the mirror on the wall, a face that had haunted him for a long time now. He had seen it almost every day since he was seven years old, he would see it for a second and then it would be gone; only now it was becoming clearer each time. Why now? Peter put it down to stress. *It's strange,* he thought, *the way things can play on the mind.*

Bethany was at the record shop, happily sorting vinyl into alphabetical order as The Cure played noisily in the background. She was fairly oblivious to her surroundings, until she heard a familiar voice.

"Beth, can we talk?"

She turned around and sure enough, Peter was standing there. Bethany did not really want to see or speak to him but she felt silly for it, as she had no real reason not to.

"Dude, I'm at work," she said, nervously running a hand through her hair. It had been dyed black and her clothes matched, her T-shirt was tighter than usual and gave her a cleavage. Peter could not help but stare.

"I know you're working now," he said, trying to look her in the eye. "I meant can we talk later?"

Bethany sighed, she resigned herself to the fact that they would have to talk eventually, and she figured that it would be better sooner rather than later. After all, there was probably a perfectly reasonable explanation. At least she hoped there was.

"I finish at six," she said. "I have to close up. Come back then."

Peter smiled, glad that she would hear him out, he just had to figure out what he was going to tell her. They had not seen each other for a fortnight. As Bethany closed up the shop, the two of them talked in a more constrained manner than they were used to. Alex's story had been all over the newspapers for nearly a week; just another case of a young life wasted. That was all forgotten when the next newsworthy tragedy happened. Nobody had seen Natalie since the event; she had left the police station and apparently disappeared.

Peter and Bethany ascended The Watch and stopped about halfway, they settled down in the long grass. They sat in awkward silence for a while, each hoping that the other would make the first move. Eventually, Peter reasoned that it should be him.

"Listen, I'm sorry..." He did not know what else to say. Bethany sighed and gave him the nudge he needed.

"Why on Earth do you have a thing like that in your home?" she asked.

"It's not mine..." Peter thought about his words carefully, should he tell her the truth?

It was not a point in his life he relished reliving. “I've told you about my dad being in prison?”

“Yeah,” Bethany replied. “You didn't tell me much. Did he kill a patient or something?” She knew that was not what happened, but Peter was never good at talking about things, so Bethany was quick to start making wild guesses.

“We were burgled,” Peter said. “A shot was fired, the guy died. Dad went down for manslaughter.”

“Where did your dad get a gun from?” Bethany asked, instantly realising that it was probably a stupid question.

“It wasn't his...” Peter told her.

“That still doesn't explain why you have a gun sitting in your drawer!” Bethany protested, Peter was becoming agitated by her interruptions.

“Would you just let me tell you what happened?!” Peter snapped, immediately regretting his abruptness. “Sorry,” he murmured. He thought Bethany had looked offended, but she seemed all right now. Perhaps he had imagined it.

“I was seven when it happened,” Peter continued. “Mum was pregnant and badly hurt – she lost the baby. Dad was just defending us, he didn't mean for the gun to go off." Peter paused for a moment, for the first time that evening Bethany had ceased asking questions and gave him her undivided attention. He went on: "While my dad called the police, I took the gun and hid it. For some stupid reason I thought that would be the end of our troubles, but everything turned to shit after that."

They sat momentarily silent, Bethany slowly taking in what he had just told her. Far from putting her at ease, it just raised more questions. Peter could tell that she wanted to ask more, but he stopped her.

"Beth, I really don't like talking about this," he said, "can we drop it?"

Bethany sighed. Lighting up a cigarette, she considered everything for a moment. Could she accept Peter's word knowing that it was not the whole truth? It would not have been the first time. Peter watched her thoughtfully, he was tired of all the secrets and lies, and there was no real reason to keep them.

"It was Mum's," he said quickly.

"What?" Bethany looked at Peter, she wondered if she had heard him correctly.

"We were protecting Mum," he replied. "She could have gone to prison for owning a gun without a licence."

Bethany raised an eyebrow and regarded Peter for a moment.

"Dude, why couldn't you just tell me that in the first place?"

He shrugged. "You didn't give me much of a chance."

Bethany recalled finding the weapon, when all manner of thoughts ran through her head. All the things that she dreamt up meant that she could not be around Peter, so she fled. She regretted that now, and was glad that he had sought her out to set things straight.

"And you're still hiding that thing, even after all this time?" she asked, then added as an afterthought: "Even after you moved house?!"

Peter smiled, more from the irony that out of amusement. "At first I buried the damn thing in the garden," he replied, "but when Mum and I were forced to move away, I dug it up and took it with me. I was a stupid kid," he added, "I didn't know what to do. I couldn't risk anyone else finding it." Peter began to laugh a little. "Actually," he said, "I can't believe mum never found it."

Bethany smiled at him but remained silent. Peter regarded her, becoming concerned.

"Are you okay?" he asked.

Bethany did not answer at first; she sat quietly, staring at the ground, processing all the new information. Finally, she looked Peter in the eye and asked: "Are *you* okay?"

"I don't understand." Peter furrowed his brow, why had she thrown his question back at him?

"There's just one thing that's worrying me," she said.

"What is it?" he asked.

"It's probably nothing..." she trailed off and stared into the distance, wondering if she was making something out of nothing.

"Tell me." Peter put his hand on her should and she looked at him again.

"There are times when I've stayed at your place," Bethany continued, "when I've heard you talking in your sleep."

Peter look shocked and scared, he took his hand sharply away from her shoulder. "Shit," he whispered. "I didn't know I did that."

"I thought you were just a sleep-talker," Bethany replied, "but now I wonder if there's something wrong?"

"What kind of things do I say?" Peter frowned.

Bethany shrugged. "You don't make a lot of sense to be honest."

She could not often pick out sentences, she

explained, only ever heard incoherent ramblings from the next room. Peter seemed relieved to hear this.

"I used to talk in my sleep when I was a kid," he said. "I had some fucked up dreams, I guess after Mum died it just brought it all back."

"I'm sorry," Bethany said, wishing she had not dragged it up. "What are your dreams about?"

"I don't know," Peter replied, "I never remember them." He looked at Bethany who stared back at him with a furrowed brow. "There's no need to worry," he said. "I'm fine." She did not seem convinced. "I'll be fine," he repeated.

Bethany looked away again, she could tell her friend was not 'fine', but there had been many times when she was too stubborn to admit that there was a problem. She knew not to push him, it would only make things worse. Bethany tried to think of something else to say, to change the subject, but she could think of nothing. The silence that grew between them was torture for her, worsened by the fact that she was unable to break it. Eventually, Peter surprised her by opening up.

"You know, sometimes I hate my parents

for not being here," he said. "My mother's dead and my father's paying for protecting his family. That makes me angry and sometimes that anger is directed at them, then I hate myself for thinking that."

Frowning, Bethany watched as her friend tortured himself, she knew exactly how he felt. "Pete, you can't hate yourself for that."

"I can," he replied, "and I will." Seeing the slight smile on his lips, Bethany could tell that Peter was at least half-joking.

"You're an idiot." She shook her head, giggling a little.

"Takes one to know one," Peter replied. Bethany gave him a swift but painless slap on the arm and then they laughed. It had been a long time since they had laughed together; things seemed normal again.

"So, I take it we're still friends?" Peter asked after a while.

"Of course we are, Pete," Bethany replied. "I'm sorry I got so freaked out."

"You don't have to apologise," he said. "I don't blame you for running off."

Bethany just shrugged; the whole thing seemed silly now. She was sure that one day, they would laugh about it. Finishing her cigarette, Bethany flicked the butt away and watched it bounce several times down the hill. Peter watched her intently.

"I'd hate to lose you as a friend, Bethany," he said. She looked at him and smiled.

"Dude, you're being melodramatic," she replied. Peter smiled too, but it was the truth, she was his closest friend and life would have been unbearable if he had not met her.

1991

Peter had moved to this strange new neighbourhood a few weeks ago. He was far away from the places and people he knew. His mother had urged him to go out and make new friends, but that was easier said than done. Peter was a shy boy and the behaviour of the other children did nothing to put him at ease.

Sean Reilly was the worst of them all, he had an instant and irrational hatred of Peter, and whatever Sean did, the children followed. They called him 'Jungle Boy' - amongst other things. The comments were confusing, inaccurate, and relentless. Peter had never experienced this in the suburbs, but in these small towns, things seemed to be different. He found it hard to get along with anyone, especially Sean and his group of friends.

In this small town it was difficult to avoid people, no matter how hard one tried. Peter walked alone, along the foot of The Watch, hands in his pockets, kicking up autumn leaves. He was in a little world of his own when he suddenly became aware that he was not alone. He looked up and there they were – Sean and his brainless cronies.

They stood in a silent stalemate for a while. Peter and Sean glared mutual hatred at one another. Peter noticed that they had their bikes with them, which would make it difficult to outrun them. Usually the gang would form a circle and hurl abuse at him - that did not seem to be happening today, though. They just stared at him, Peter, on his own against Sean with four of his friends. One of the group Peter recognised as Natalie, the others, all boys, he had never seen before

As usual, it was Sean who lead the name-calling.

"What are you looking at, Monkey Boy?" he sneered. The other children sniggered. Peter just frowned, he did not know why they hated him so much, nor did he know why he just stood there, silently taking the abuse.

Why don't you say something back? *He*

asked himself.

"Yeah, what are you looking at?" ventured one of the other boys. "Stop staring or we'll kick the shit out of you."

"Nah, you don't want to touch him!" said Sean. "You might catch one of his jungle diseases." The other laughed with the exception of Natalie, who tugged at Sean's sleeve.

"Just leave him alone," she said.

Peter continued to glare, he could not believe that people could be so pathetic and ignorant. They singled him out because he was different, Peter decided it was time to focus on the one thing that made Sean different. What he was about to say was either very brave, or very stupid.

"Fuck you, ginger nut!"

The group stopped laughing and stared at him for a second. They looked ready to pounce. Peter turned and ran. Over the last few weeks he had become good at running. He sprinted along a path ascending the hill, if he could just make it into the woods...

Peter could hear the group on their bikes, gaining on him. If he could reach the trees he could lose them and make his escape, if not, there was a distinct possibility that he was going to die that day.

Reaching the edge of the woods, Peter halted. There were three other children there, two girls and a boy. Sean's friends? No, from the way everyone stopped and stared, he could see that the two groups had a mutual dislike of each other.

"Get lost!" Sean yelled, waving his arm as though to shoo them away. "This has nothing to do with you."

"We were here first." The boy shrugged. "You get lost."

Sean glared while Peter stood catching his breath, relieved that the attention was no longer solely on him.

"You don't want that hanging around, do you?" Sean was pointing at Peter. The small, mousey-haired girl looked from Peter to Sean.

"He's with us," she said. "Take a hike."

"You can't seriously want to hang around with him?!" Sean protested.

"Piss off, Sean!" the girl yelled. He stayed where he was. Incensed that Sean was not getting the message, the girl grabbed a small rock and hurled it at him, hitting him square in the shoulder and knocking him of his bicycle. Natalie failed to suppress a snigger.

Sean picked himself up, and he and his group of friends withdrew, shouting various, empty threats as they did so. The mousey-haired girl turned to Peter and smiled.

"Hi," she said, and then gestured to the other two children there. "That's Kevin and Karen, and my name's Bethany."

Still sat in the long grass on the hill, Peter watched Bethany as she attempted to light another cigarette, but the wind kept blowing her lighter out.

"I'm glad I met you," he said. "Kevin and Karen too. I think I would hate it here if I didn't know you."

"It's a small town," she replied, still struggling with her lighter. "You would have met us at some point."

"You know what I mean," Peter said, feeling she may have missed the point. "Having you guys around made things easier," he continued. "It was bad enough having to leave home, but then we moved here, where no one knew us but everyone seemed to have a problem with the colour of our skin."

Bethany finally succeeded in lighting her cigarette and smiled triumphantly. Peter wondered if she had been listening.

"Hmm..." Bethany took a long drag then

blew a smoke ring. “This town is a lot more diverse than it used to be,” she said. “Kids didn't know any better back then. Not that that makes it right, of course.”

They sat together silently for a while, but not awkward like before, each enjoying the company of the other. Bethany lay back in the grass, Peter followed suit and they looked up at the sky as it slowly began to turn orange.

“It's getting dark,” he said after a while. “we can't stay up here all night.”

Bethany shrugged. “I'm not ready to go home yet.” She took another long drag from her cigarette and lay silently watching the sun set. It was some time before she spoke. “I'm glad I met you too, Pete.”

“Glad to hear it,” he replied.

“You're the glue that holds the group together.”

Peter laughed. “You think so?”

“Oh, I know so!” Bethany giggled, then letting her smile fade, she added: “I doubt Kevin and I would still be friends if it wasn't for you.”

Peter looked at her and perked an eyebrow, he found that hard to believe.

“After my accident I found it difficult to be around him,” she explained. “He'd just lost his sister and I had just lost my family."

Both she and Peter had been there when Karen died, and that had been bad enough. Bethany could not have imagined what it was like to see a family member die, until a few months later, when her parent's car crashed, leaving her the sole survivor. Instead of feeling empathy for each other, Kevin and Bethany withdrew into themselves. Looking back, she figured that they had both been too young and selfish to know how to deal with their grief; they never talked about it, partly through fear of upsetting the other and partly because they did not wish to acknowledge the other's pain when trying to deal with their own. Bethany knew she was guiltier of the latter, sometimes feeling that her grief outweighed his, even going as far as resenting him because he had only lost one relative and not three.

"They say misery loves company," Bethany continued, "but I hated being around people – especially someone who was equally as miserable." She took another long drag from her cigarette then added: "That sounds pretty selfish, doesn't it?"

"That doesn't make you a bad person, Beth," Peter sighed. "You guys are okay now, I'm sure it was all just part of the grieving process."

"I guess." Bethany shrugged. "Sometimes I do feel like a bad person."

"Why?" Peter sat up and stared down at her, for a while Bethany just stared up at the sky and did not answer.

Sitting up, Bethany threw away her cigarette butt and met Peter's gaze.

"Sometimes I feel guilty," she said at last. "I feel like I shouldn't be here, that I should have died in that crash with my brother and my parents."

Peter grimaced. "You know I don't like it when you talk like that." He had heard her say these things before; she had a strange sense of guilt and if anything bad happened Bethany often thought she deserved it. Peter had a hard job trying to convince her otherwise.

"Sometimes I see them," she said, "my parents."

Peter raised his eyebrows and Bethany smiled awkwardly.

"I'd be walking around town, say," she continued, "and I'd catch a glimpse of my mum in the crowd. I'd turn around to get a second look, but it's someone else – who doesn't even look like Mum."

"That's not so crazy," Peter laughed.

"Sometimes when I'm in the flat on my own, I'll start talking to mum, then I remember that there's no one there but me."

Peter's smile faded as he remembered the emptiness that he often felt, but he remained thankful for his friends. He looked at Bethany and noticed that she was shivering. The sky was almost black now and the air had turned cold. Peter surrendered his jacket to her, Bethany smiled and accepted it. It was her favourite jacket of his – dark, brown suede and very comfortable, even if it was a little large for her.

"So," said Bethany, as she wrapped the jacket around her, "we're both crazy."

Peter smiled. "All the best people are." Then in a more serious tone, he added: "Don't torture yourself, Beth."

She frowned and shrugged. "I don't really mean the things I say. It's just... you know..." Bethany found it hard to find to words to describe how she was feeling, but Peter understood.

"I know," he said.

Looking at the street below, Bethany thought that it was time they moved along, she glanced over at Peter and noticed that he was shaking slightly.

"Now you're cold, aren't you?" she asked.

“Fucking freezing,” he replied.

Bethany laughed, there was no way she was going to relinquish the jacket now. “Do you want to get something to eat?” she asked.

“That's the most intelligent thing I've heard all evening.” Peter said as he patted Bethany on the shoulder. She let out a sharp cry of pain. Peter did not have to ask what was wrong with her, he already knew; there would be times when Bethany would wear different attire or many more wristbands than was usual for her. Sometimes she would use other means to cover up a burn, a bruise or any other kind of injury.

“Beth,” Peter sighed, “you shouldn't let him get away with that.”

9.
Brian

1994

"Are you excited to be going home Bethany?" the nurse asked the little girl, who just nodded unenthusiastically.

"Brian's here to take you home," chirped the social worker, who had arrived with Bethany's uncle, her mother's brother. "Are you looking forward to staying with your uncle?" she continued. "It'll be good to get out of here, won't it?"

The social worker, Suzanne, had visited Bethany several times during her stay in the hospital, and Bethany could neither stand her nor her patronising tone of voice.

"I guess so." The little girl shrugged. She had become used to the hospital having been there for some time, being treated for shock and injuries; including broken ribs. The thought of leaving for somewhere unfamiliar was unpleasant, repugnant. She was not ready to accept life without her parents.

Suzanne had been there when the doctors told Bethany that her parents had died, as had her younger brother, John. Suzanne assured her that she would be well looked after, she would live with her uncle Brian, the only family she had left. Although Bethany liked Brain this was no consolation, she wanted to be with her parents, but it had barely sunken in that she would never see them again.

Brian took Suzanne to one side. They stood whispering in the corner; Bethany could tell that they were talking about her. What was so secret that they could not talk openly in front of her?

"I don't know how to look after a kid," Brian said. "What if I can't cope?"

"Would you rather your niece go into care, Mr. Jackson?" Suzanne asked curtly.

"Well, no," Brian stammered, "of course not, but..."

"Listen, you know we're here to help as much as we can," Suzanne tried to sound as reassuring as possible. "I appreciate that you're grieving, but so is Bethany." She looked over to the little girl who sat on the bed with her arms folded, scowling. "She's an eleven year old girl," Suzanne continued, "she needs your support."

"I know." Brian sighed and looked at his niece.

"You have got to be strong for her,"

Suzanne insisted. "You're all she has left."

"She's all I have left," Brian said to himself.

Bethany sat on the bed watching the two of them whispering. The nurse had departed and left them on their own. Every so often the whispering would stop; they would turn and look at Bethany, then turn back to continue their private conversation. Eventually, they turned to face the little girl once more.

"Are you ready to go?" Brian asked as cheerfully as he could manage.

"No," Bethany said almost inaudibly as she shook her head.

"Come on, it's time to go!" Suzanne said encouragingly, her voice only grating on Bethany's nerves.

"No!" she cried. "I want my mum!"

Bethany returned home after her dinner with Peter and quietly shut the front door behind her. He had been reluctant to let her go home, but she was adamant; there was no arguing with Bethany Matthews. It had been the cause of minor squabbles between the two; Peter had no idea why she had to be so obstinate. She wondered about that herself, sometimes.

Creeping down the hallway of the small bungalow, Bethany peered into the front room where the television set was blaring in the corner. Brian was asleep on the sofa and empty beer cans were scattered around the place. Creeping over to the sofa, so as not to disturb her uncle, Bethany reached for the remote control. She turned the sound on the television right down and wondered how he could sleep with it being so loud.

She made her way to her bedroom and, just as she reached the door, Brian called over to her. She sighed heavily and turned around to face him.

“What?” she asked.

“Where have you been?” he slurred.

“That's my business,” she said, folding her arms defensively. Brian merely grunted and turned over on his side to go back to sleep. Bethany sighed and went into her room, shutting the door behind her and bolting it.

10.
Sean

Kevin sat in Sean's front room. He knew what he wanted to say, but unsure how to say it. Sean's two year old son, Jack, was playing quietly in the corner. Lounging back in his chair, Sean fiddled with a Rubik's Cube; he had owned it since high school and had never solved it.

Sean was a tall, well-built man of twenty. His hair had darkened a little with age; he was well dressed and often considered handsome until he opened his mouth to speak.

“I get the feeling this isn't a social visit, Marshall,” he prodded as Kevin had not said anything for several minutes.

“The fact that I said I wanted to talk business may have been a give-away,” Kevin remarked, grinning. “I've been thinking about a lot of things lately,” he continued. “I don't think I can go on selling your... produce.” He quickly glanced into the corner, being careful of what he said in front of the child.

“This has something to do with Alex, doesn't it?” Sean asked flatly.

“Partly,” Kevin replied. “But it's not just

that. What if we sold him something dodgy?"

Sean stopped playing with his cube momentarily and looked as though he was in deep thought. "You know, I've asked myself that a lot," he said.

"And?" Kevin asked.

"And nothing." Sean shrugged. "I haven't heard any horror stories from any of my other clients." He paused and studied the unimpressed look that appeared on Kevin's face. "The guy was an addict," he continued, "he probably took too much and that's why he died; it wasn't your fault or anybody else's."

"How can you be so callous?" Kevin asked. "We sold him that shit, how can you not feel at least partly responsible?"

Sighing, Sean stared at Kevin for a moment before answering. "I find it's usually best not to dwell on these things," he said. "Of course I feel bad, but Alex could have got that shit from anywhere, we don't know that it came from us."

Kevin huffed in frustration; before he could speak, Sean carried on. "All I'm saying is don't blame yourself," he said. "That's all. Dwelling on it won't change a damn thing!"

Kevin nodded absently. "Even so," he said quietly. "I can't stop thinking about it. It's just one of the many reasons why I can't continue selling."

"I see," Sean replied. "Then stop selling."

"It's that easy, huh?"

"If you want it to be." Sean told him. Kevin seemed surprised that it was that simple, Sean laughed. "I'm not going to send my boys round to break your legs just because you want to stop selling for me!" he said. "You've been watching too many movies."

Kevin laughed, though half-heartedly. "So you don't mind?"

"Well, I'll be sorry to see you go," Sean replied. "just do me one last favour and we'll call it quits. How does that sound?"

"One more?" Kevin nodded and thought about it for a moment; reluctantly he accepted. One last favour would not hurt, and then he could forget about the whole thing. He would go to the club where Sean worked and receive the stash at the door. Kevin would sell off that last batch and that would be the end of it. They shook on it and it was resolved. Sean resumed playing with the Rubik's Cube.

"Would you ever give up selling?" Kevin asked after a time.

"I don't know." Sean shrugged. "It keeps a roof over my head and feeds my son;

working at the club just isn't enough."

"You could always find something better." Kevin replied.

"That's easier said than done, Marshall." Sean said, his tone becoming agitated. It was clear to Kevin that he was unwilling to discuss the subject further, so he said no more

Sean ceased fiddling with his cube, held it out in front of him and stared at it.

"I never could work this thing out." he said.

Kevin took the cube from him and tried it himself; it took him less than a minute. He handed the completed cube back to Sean, who stared at it some more.

"I've been trying to figure that out for years!" he said. Pointing a mocking finger at Kevin, he added: "You're lucky I don't kick your arse!"

Kevin laughed and replied with equal sarcasm, "You terrify me, Sean."

Heading down the high street towards the club, Kevin was beginning to regret his agreement with Sean. Tonight would be Kevin's final 'favour', after that he would be free. Free to feel guilty for which would probably be a long time, but at least he would no longer feel like a hypocrite. At least that was the idea.

His agitation increased with every step. *Just get this over and done with*, he thought. He cast a glance towards Bethany, who was walking alongside him. She was there for moral support – not that she knew it.

In an attempt to distract himself from the task that loomed ahead, Kevin decided to mock his friend's new dye job. Bethany changed hair colour every few weeks; this time it was bright orange, but the tips were still black from the last time she had dyed it. She ignored his jibes though, having heard them all before.

"Are you and Pete talking yet?" Kevin asked her.

"What makes you think we weren't?" she replied.

Kevin smiled. He could deduce from her answer that everything was fine but she was not going to talk about it. He was satisfied with that; he did not want any details, just to know that things were back to normal. Whenever any two of them fell out it always made things awkward for the third, however unintentionally. For now at least, Kevin was safe in the knowledge that the three of them could hang out and he would not have to worry about breaking up any fights.

They approached the club where Sean stood outside with another doorman.

"All right, Marshall?" he called out and walked towards them. Patting Kevin on the shoulder, Sean took him to one side where they began to talk quietly. Bethany's initial annoyance quickly dissipated; she would rather not speak to Sean if she could help it. She smiled at the other doorman and made small talk with him. She was beginning to run out of things to say when the other two strolled back over. Bethany folded her arms and scowled at Sean as he turned his attention to her.

"All right, Beth?" he asked with a leer.

"Fine, thanks," she replied flatly.

Before anyone could utter another word, she ushered Kevin into the club. Once through the door they were hit with a wall of hot, sticky air; metal was blaring through the sound system, making the floor and walls vibrate. Bliss.

They headed straight for the bar, where they ordered beer, having to yell at the barman to be heard over the music. Across the room, Bethany spotted a familiar face.

"Lucas!" she shouted, bouncing up and down, and waving with both arms to get his attention. He smiled and made his way over.

Lucas worked with Bethany at the record shop. He was roughly Kevin's height but with a slightly larger build. People who did not know them so well had often confused one for the other until Lucas began growing his hair into dreadlocks. Kevin had always liked Lucas, seeing him as one of the few genuinely friendly people in town, he had even sold to him on a couple of occasions. It was a thought which reminded him...

A couple of hours had passed and the evening had not been entirely successful, but was not a total loss either. Kevin had now sold around half of what Sean had given him on the door, he would wait until the next wave of people came flooding through the door, then circulate the room again. In the meantime, he stood and chatted to Lucas and Bethany, beginning to enjoy himself until Lucas drew his attention to something.

“I don't want to worry you Kev, but...” he nodded towards the exit. Kevin looked over his shoulder to see a police woman in full uniform. She appeared to be asking for something – or some*one*.

“Fuck!” he hissed. “What if she finds this stuff on me?! I'm going to be in deep shit!”

“Don't panic!” said Bethany. “Sneak out

through the window in the bathroom, I'll meet you outside."

"There *is* no window in the men's toilets." Kevin protested.

"Oh, for goodness sake!" Bethany rolled her eyes and grabbing Kevin by the arm, pulled him through the crowd, briefly looking back over her shoulder to wave goodbye to Lucas. He waved back and laughed to himself.

They fought their way through the throng to the back of the club and through to the ladies' bathroom. Initially there were protests to Kevin being there, but then Bethany yelled: "Quick! Get the window open!" Realising that it was an emergency, one of the girls opened the window while two others, who had been rolling a joint, hastily stuffed their stash into their bras. Many women had made their escape through that window over the years, either to elude the bouncers or to get away from a drunken nuisance who did not understand the meaning of the word 'no'.

Kevin was ushered out first, he had to climb up onto a basin and crawl out through the window, which was a tight squeeze. Bethany looked fretfully over her shoulder towards the door. Kevin slowly scaled down a drain-pipe and landed just outside the service entrance at the back of the club. Bethany was behind him within seconds, landing neatly on her feet, she had clearly done this before.

After laying low for a while, they sneaked quietly out of the alleyway and looked down the street. There were just the two bouncers at the door of the club, which was good. Kevin and Bethany walked in the opposite direction, trying to look as inconspicuous as possible. As quickly and calmly as they could, they made their way towards The Watch, but someone had caught up with them and tapped them on their shoulders. Whipping around, they saw that it was Lucas.

"Christ!" said Bethany. "You scared the crap out of me!"

Kevin stood there silently, the colour drained from his face.

"Sorry guys," Lucas smirked, "but I had to come and tell you there was nothing to worry about." His grin broadened, as though he were about to reveal the punchline to a joke that only Kevin and Bethany had not heard before. "You know it was someone's birthday...?" he continued.

"What?" Kevin said impatiently.

"That WPC in there," Lucas jutted his thumb in the direction of the club, "that was a stripper."

Kevin did not look in the slightest bit amused. Lucas tried to stifle back a snigger while Bethany burst out laughing.

Kevin shook his head in disbelief. "All that drama for nothing!" He glared at Bethany; who was still doubled up in hysterics. "I climbed out of the window," he continued, "in the girls' toilets, to make an escape from a fucking stripper!" Bethany laughed even harder, she sounded like she was hyperventilating.

"Stop!" she wheezed, "You're killing me!" After a few moments, Bethany's laughter had subsided a little, although each time it looked like she was going to stop, she started again. Kevin shrugged. "I guess we can go back inside, then," he said. "Get a few more beers in."

"I don't know," Lucas replied. "I'd say Beth's had enough!" She laughed louder and harder than before, but calmed down much quicker this time.

"No, dudes," she said. "I've got a better idea."

The three of them sat in the long grass of the hill, watching what little traffic was going by that late at night. Bethany was still breaking out into occasional, spasmodic giggles. Even Kevin had started to see the funny side of things, either that or Bethany's laughter was contagious. They neared the end of the joint that they had been passing around between them.

"I should head off in a sec," said Lucas. "Some of us have work in the morning."

"Yeah, me too," Bethany agreed. "I could do with an early night. Well," she added, "early*ish*."

Kevin drew on the last of the joint and threw the butt away. He had the luxury of a morning off, so he thought he would stay out a little longer, and head up to the promenade on The Watch.

"You do enjoy sitting up on that Watch by yourself," Bethany remarked. Kevin just shrugged.

"Maybe he has a secret girlfriend up there." Lucas grinned. This was greeted by silence. Bethany laughed.

"Lucas, I think you're right!" she exclaimed. Kevin flushed as they prodded and teased him further.

"Leave me alone..." he mumbled with a sly smile fixed on his face.

"Oh, come on," Bethany nudged him playfully. "You know we're only teasing."

Lucas got to his feet and helped Bethany

up, she staggered and giggled. He offered to walk with her as far as the high street. They bid Kevin good-night, with Bethany adding: “Let's leave him to his mystery woman!” She then proceeded to make kissing noises. Kevin grinned and slowly raised his middle finger. He watched them walk away as he lit a cigarette, Bethany was swaying slightly and hung on to Lucas' arm for support. Kevin got up from the grass and ascended The Watch towards the promenade.

Deep within the trees and bushes that adorned the church yard, Natalie sat on the ground below the weeping willow where she and Alex had spent much of their time. He was sitting just behind her. Both stared off into the distance.

“It should have been you, not me.” Alex said.

“Yes,” Natalie agreed.

11.
Too Close for Comfort

Kevin reached the promenade to see that Karen was already there. They always seemed to be there at the same time, when there was no one else around; it was as though she knew when Kevin would be alone, when he needed the company of someone who understood him. He met the girl little more than two weeks ago, but he felt as though he had known her for an entire lifetime. He *knew* her. She knew him. It was almost telepathic.

Karen stood absent-mindedly staring up at the statue of Gabriel. She appeared to be in deep contemplation.

"Penny for your thoughts?" said Kevin. She started and smiled as she saw him.

"Marshall!" She hugged him. "I had a feeling I'd see you!" Kevin hugged her back and held on to her for a lingering moment. She smelled sweet. Karen felt good to him somehow; felt right. She had her arms tightly around his waist; she looked up at him with her smiling eyes.

"How are you?" she asked.

"All the better for seeing you," he replied.

Karen smiled up at him and he kissed her lightly on the cheek.

Bethany strolled downhill towards home. She had said goodbye to Lucas at the top of the high street, and she did not have too far left to walk. Breathing in the cold night air, she was beginning to feel wide-awake and sober. Hearing her name called from across the street, Bethany turned to see Sean coming towards her. She rolled her eyed and carried on walking as Sean paced quickly behind her.

"I heard all about your daring escape earlier," he said with a grin. "I wish I'd been there to see it."

"I'll bet."

"Where's Kevin now," he continued, "does he have what he owes me?"

Bethany huffed and walked faster. "I'm not his keeper, Sean."

Taking her entirely by surprise, Sean grabbed Bethany by the arm, pushed her up against a wall and stood over her, placing his hands on the wall either side of her.

"Listen," he snarled, "that friend of yours has dropped me in the shit this week." Bethany stared at him, wide-eyed, momentarily paralysed. "I want what he owes me," he continued, "and I want you to pass this little message on for me, okay?"

Before Bethany could react, Sean had his hand under her T-shirt and had slipped something into her bra. She flinched and tried to push him away but he gripped her arms, pinching her skin. She gritted her teeth, not wanting to give him the satisfaction of knowing he was hurting her.

"Let's get one thing straight," he hissed into her ear, his sickly breath on her neck nauseating her. "This is over when I say it is."

Bethany remained motionless and many minutes seemed to go by before Sean let go of her arms.

"Give my regards to Marshall, won't you?" He looked down at her with a satisfied smile, and then pulled away. Bethany stood and stared for a few seconds as Sean walked back the way he had come. Shaking, she turned and made her way towards home, looking back over her shoulder to make sure that Sean was not coming back. Quickening her pace with each step, she eventually broke into a run.

Bethany slipped in through the side door into her kitchen. She poured herself a glass of water, downed it and shuddered, slamming the glass down onto the counter. Sean made her skin crawl – now more so than ever. With the confrontation still fresh in her mind, Bethany dug into her bra, reaching for whatever it was that Sean had put there. She held it in her hand for a moment, a plastic bag full of pills. She had no idea what they were and did not want to know. She refused to get involved. Emptying the packet into the sink, she turned on the tap and drained them.

Looking around the kitchen, Bethany saw that it was a complete mess. Wherever Brian went he seemed to leave a trail of filth. *Like a slug*, Bethany thought. There were beer cans everywhere, dirty dishes and an ashtray overflowing with cigarette butts. She could not deal with that now, she would have to clean it up in the morning.

1996

Bethany had just returned home from school, and shutting the front door, she glanced over at Brian who was sat on the sofa, staring at the television. He had clearly been drinking; she could smell the alcohol from where she stood it the doorway. It was not the first time that Bethany had seen her uncle that way.

"What?!" he said, looking up at her. She had not realised that she had been staring in a disapproving manner. She turned away and tried to make it to the safety of her room, but Brian was too quick. He grabbed Bethany by the arm and flung her to the floor, sitting astride her, he pinned her arms down with his knees.

Having no idea what had just happened, Bethany lay there in a blind panic; unable to move, unable to speak, time seemed to slow down. Her uncle took a long drag from his cigarette and blew the smoke into her face. Looking down at his niece with a blank expression, Brian took hold of Bethany by the chin to keep her head still and slowly brought his cigarette down towards her forehead.

She screamed and struggled, but in vain. It seemed to happen so slowly that she could see it edging closer by the millimetre, but she could not escape it. She felt the heat before it even touched her skin.

Bethany absent-mindedly rubbed the small, round scar on her forehead, when she was startled by a loud crash coming from the front room. Her uncle was home. She sighed heavily and decided it would be best to lock herself in her room, but as she turned to leave the kitchen, she saw that Brian was already blocking the doorway. She glared at him while he stared blankly at her.

"I see her every time I look at you." he sneered.

"What?" Bethany sighed wearily and folded her arms.

"You heard," Brian slurred. "You're more like your mother every day. I don't like it."

Bethany did not like it either. She saw her mother whenever she looked in the mirror and she did not need to be reminded of it. Pushing past him into the hallway, Bethany walked quickly towards her room. Brian staggered after her, leaning against the wall for support. "Don't walk away from me when..."

"Piss off, Brian!" she yelled as she pushed her bedroom door open.

"...When I'm trying to talk to you." Brian finished as he stumbled up to Bethany's door, which was swiftly slammed in his face.

Once inside, Bethany slid the bolt across. Brian banged loudly. "Open this door!" he yelled, and banged again. Leaning with her back against the door, she could feel it shaking from her uncle's incessant pounding. She slid down and sat on the floor with her knees up against her chest, the banging at the door did not let up, neither did the continual profanities coming from Brian's mouth; she feared that if he did not stop, he would soon break the door down. As silent tears streamed down her face, Bethany grabbed her mobile and dialled Peter's number. It just kept on ringing.

Please pick up, she thought. *Please*.

12.
Clinging On

1996

Imogen Crossgrave returned home from work. Peter was already there and, as usual, so was Bethany. Imogen did not dislike Bethany - she thought she was a sweet girl - but sometimes she felt as though she had two children instead of just one. At least they were sensible children, she would always come home to find they had completed their homework and were watching the television, or reading, or in this case, talking quietly.

Peter and Bethany sat at the kitchen counter, and when Imogen walked into the room they stopped discussing whatever it was that was so secretive. The girl turned on the charm, as usual. "Hello Mrs. Crossgrave," she chirped. "How are you?" Imogen could not help but smile back. She greeted both children cheerfully, Peter just smiled; he was being quiet, even for him. Switching the kettle on; Imogen started to make tea, she looked up at the clock on the wall.

"Shouldn't you be going home soon, Bethany?" she asked. "It's getting dark."

"Can't she stay?" Peter asked quickly. Imogen raised an eyebrow and looked from her son to Bethany, who had begun to bite her thumbnail, it was a nervous habit she had developed.

"Won't your uncle be getting worried?" she asked.

Bethany shrugged. "He won't care."

Imogen sighed. "Tell you what," she said. "Why don't you stay for dinner, then I'll drive you home, okay?" Bethany grinned broadly and thanked her, then turned to smile at Peter. The girl had ceased biting her nail and rested her elbow on the counter: that was when Imogen noticed the mark on her wrist.

"That's a nasty bruise you have there," she said. Bethany looked down at her arms and swiftly moved them to rest in her lap. She looked up and said: "I fell on it."

Peter looked at her despairingly, but Bethany just shrugged at him. However long she stayed, it would not be long enough, and soon she would have to go back 'home'.

Peter got home later than usual; he made straight for his room and sat down on the bed, pulling off his shoes. He stayed there for a while, resting his head in his hands, these late nights – or early mornings - would be the death of him. He took of his jacket and after retrieving his mobile from the pocket, he threw it over the back of the chair in the corner. His mobile had been set to silent all night, and looking at the screen, Peter saw that he had four missed calls from Bethany. It was too late to call her back now; he would have to speak to her in the morning.

Placing his mobile on the bedside table, Peter felt a shiver go through him. A sickly chill had begun radiating from the chair where he had thrown his jacket. Turning his gaze towards to it, Peter saw the stranger sitting there; the stranger he had caught glimpses of every day for twelve years, and was becoming clearer each time.

Why now? Was he seeing this man out of guilt? No, he was seeing things a long time before he felt guilty. Perhaps he was going insane – this was not the only manifestation he ever saw. Peter stared directly into the eyes of the man who had broken into his home all those years ago.

"What do you want?" he asked evenly.

"I don't want anything," the man replied, "you're the one who keeps me here."

Peter pulled a face and looked away; he was too tired to be dealing in riddles. He sighed and shook his head; he did not want to keep going through this. “Why, after all this time,” he asked, “are you still here?”

“I'm here,” the stranger replied, “because you won't let it go.”

Peter glared at him. Of course he could not let it go, this man had torn his family apart. His father had been in prison for ten years and would likely be there for ten more. His mother had not been in her grave a year; she had an aneurysm, caused by the blow to the head during the burglary – twelve years later, it had ruptured and killed her. Peter often resented being on his own, which left him feeling guilty; this would quickly turn to anger, which would be directed towards the one person who had caused it all – everything pointed back to the stranger sat in front of him.

“What do you want me to say?” The man threw his arms out in a shrug. “Tell you how sorry I am? I've tried talking to you before, but you never listened.”

Peter grunted. He had no idea why he was listening to the man now. Standing up, he began to pace the room.

“Do you even give a toss about what you put my family through?” Peter stopped to glare down at the man sitting in the chair, who merely shrugged.

"I won't beg you for forgiveness," he replied. "I won't need it where I'm going."

Peter sat back down and the two stared at each other for a moment.

"I never meant for anyone to get hurt," the man said at last. "That's the truth."

"Well, they did." Peter replied quietly. The stranger sighed and leaned back in the chair with his arms folded. He regarded Peter for some time. Why hold on to one moment from the past?

"Why not just accept things for the way they are?" he asked. Peter continued to stare at his unwanted guest and still said nothing. The stranger smiled knowingly and rephrased his question. "Why not accept yourself for who *you* are?"

Peter felt his eye twitch. He was trying as hard as he could not to show the utter contempt he was feeling. The last thing he wanted was advice from the man who had destroyed a large part of his life. The worst thing about it was the fact that he was right, there was nothing Peter could do to change a single thing. He had to let it go.

"I think there's something seriously wrong with me," Peter said to himself, resting his head in his hand.

"You can believe that all you like," the stranger replied, "or you can choose to deal things as they are."

Peter looked up and glared at him. Who was this man to keep giving him advice? Was it an attempt to make up for his past deeds? That did not make a lot of sense to Peter. The stranger did not seem particularly remorseful, yet he had already alluded to the fact that he had accepted he was going to Hell. Peter believed in neither Paradise nor eternal damnation – was his visitor's belief in it enough? Ever since the incident, Peter had wanted justice, and there was none. His parents had suffered because of it, and in turn, so had he. Had the stranger lived, then he would be in prison and Peter's father would not. His mother may still have been hurt...

Sighing heavily, Peter stood up and faced away from his unwanted guest. He had to stop doing this to himself, running through every possible scenario in his mind. Folding his arms, Peter looked up at the ceiling as though the answer was written there.

"I want you to go," he said at last. Holding on to that point in his life was doing more harm than good, and Peter knew it.

"Just go," he repeated as he turned around

to face the stranger, but he had already gone.

Peter never saw that man's face again.

Arriving at the record shop where Bethany worked, Kevin discovered that she was there alone. Perfect. He looked around to make especially sure that there was no one else there. It had been a quiet morning and Bethany sat behind the counter with a bored expression on her face, drumming her fingers on the counter's top. She smiled when she saw Kevin, which surprised her as she had been deliberately avoiding him for the past few days.

"I spoke to Sean yesterday," Kevin said, he noticed Bethany's smile drop. "He said he gave you something to pass onto me?"

Bethany shuddered at the thought of Sean's hands on her, and she made no effort to answer her friend's question. Kevin knew that Sean had slipped her drugs - what they were exactly he was not sure. He was disgusted with the lengths Sean would go to to stay in control, Bethany should not have been involved - Kevin should have never got involved.

"It's all right, Beth," he said, "just give whatever it is to me and I'll take it back. This isn't your fight." Bethany leaned on the counter and looked at Kevin, her expression made him dread what she was about to say.

"Sorry..." she whispered.

Kevin sighed and stared at her, he was going to need more information than that. He locked eyes with her until she continued. "Sean slipped me some pills the other night," she said. "I don't know what they were; I chucked them down the sink." She watched as Kevin paled and slowly shook his head. "I didn't know what else to do," she added. "I'm sorry."

"Fuck!" he said, raising his hands to his head and staring at a fixed spot just behind Bethany as though a monster were hovering over her shoulder. "Sean's gonna have me for this." He continued to stare silently for a moment before angrily looking her in the eye again. "Do you have any idea what you've done Bethany?" he asked. "Do you?!"

"I'm sorry," she repeated meekly.

"Sorry just won't cut it," Kevin snapped bitterly. "What the fuck were you thinking?!" He began to pace furiously in the small space in front of the counter, Bethany stood by quietly, not knowing what else to say.

As Kevin continued to pace, uttering the odd profanity, Bethany feared he would wear a hole in the floor. “Marshall...”

“I'm sorry, Beth,” he said, shaking his head. “but I can't talk to you right now.” Kevin turned and stormed out of the shop, she called after him but a second later, he was gone.

Bethany sighed; she would have to try to talk to him later, when he had had time to calm down. She knew that what she had done was stupid, but she had acted on impulse. Sean and Kevin's relationship had been tenuous at best and now Bethany worried for her friend's safety. In the back of her mind she worried about her own – she knew that Sean would not go easy on her.

Stepping out from behind the counter, Bethany watched the door. She felt a chill in the air and moved to close it to stop the draught. Shutting the door, she was sure she saw some movement out of the corner of her eye and immediately shrugged it off – she had been lacking in sleep lately, and her mind was likely playing tricks on her. She saw it again. Strange, Bethany thought she had been alone in the shop, but she could see the movement of shadows coming from the office.

“Lucas?” she called. “Is that you?” She march to the back of the shop and pushed open the office door to see that there was no one there, Bethany suddenly felt very cold. Perhaps she was coming down with something. She shivered and closed the door to the office before returning to the counter. Bethany sat down and waited for her shift to be over.

Kevin sat at his desk, engrossed in his work. He heard the sound of someone being let into the house and directed upstairs. There was a knock at his door and Bethany appeared in the doorway.

"Can I come in?" she asked tentatively. Kevin smiled and gestured for her to come inside. Bethany shut the door behind her and walked over to the desk, where she perched on the corner.

"You've changed your hair again!" Kevin remarked. It was a little shorter than before, and now electric blue. "Don't you worry that it'll fall out one day?" he added.

"Fuck off, dude." Bethany laughed. She had kept her distance from Kevin for a few days, but now she concluded that he had had sufficient time to calm down, and she was ready to clear the air.

"I'm sorry I flushed those pills, Kev," she

said. “I just panicked.”

“No, I'm the one who should apologise, Sean shouldn't have got you involved.” Kevin sighed as he realised that he had not even asked her if she was all right. “He didn't hurt you, did he?”

Bethany shrugged and shook her head. She had had worse. “Have you spoken to him yet?” she asked.

“No!” Kevin sniggered and shook his head. The prospect of seeing Sean was amusing and terrifying in equal measures. “I've been avoiding him,” he said in a more serious tone. “I'll have to face him soon, though.”

“We can face him together, if you like,” Bethany suggested.

“No,” Kevin replied, “like I said, this isn't your fight.”

Bethany readily accepted that refusal. She was brave but she was not stupid. Scanning the desk, she took in some of Kevin's drawings – all were images of angels. The subject of each picture looked familiar, but Bethany could not put a name to the face. “They're pretty,” she said absently as she picked up one of the drawings to study it more closely. “What are you working on?”

Kevin shrugged. “Just a project.”

Placing the picture back on the desk, some photographs caught Bethany's eye. She picked one up for closer inspection. Karen. She looked around eight years old, the picture must have been taken the summer just before the accident. Bethany shuddered.

"You still keep all these photos?" she asked.

"Yeah," Kevin nodded. "As long as I keep remembering her, it's as though she's still here in some way."

Bethany smiled, she had not thought of things that way. She had spent much of her time trying not to remember. Kevin was looking at another photograph. "Sometimes I worry that I'll forget what she looked like," he continued. "So I keep these pictures of her close by." He looked up at Bethany. "That sounds a bit weird, doesn't it?"

"No," Bethany smiled. "That doesn't sound weird at all."

She handed the photograph back to Kevin, and he stared at it for a while.

"Do you still have pictures of your family?" he asked.

"A few," she shrugged. "I tend not to look at old photos, it's too painful." Bethany thought of the hundreds of family photographs that lay hidden in a box in the cupboard. She wondered if she would ever look at them again.

13.
For Survival

1994

Bianca Matthews had a headache. She was driving her family home after a long, irritating day, and the two children in the back seat would not stop fighting.

"Mum!" Bethany complained. "John's making faces at me!"

"For goodness sake!" Bianca snapped. "We're nearly home. Can't you two give it a rest for a few minutes?!"

"You heard your mother." Andrew turned round in his seat to scold his children. "You kids just behave."

They drove along the foot of The Watch and Bianca glanced in the rear-view mirror at the children in the back, who remained sulkily silent. Bethany glanced over at John, who poked his tongue out at her. She slapped him. Bianca caught sight of this and turned round. "Bethany!" she yelled. "He's half your age, just leave him alone!"

"He's not leaving me alone!" Bethany slumped back into her seat with her arms folded, scowling.

Andrew shook his wife by the shoulder, bringing her attention back to the road. A girl stood in their path and made no attempt to move out of the way. Panicking, Bianca swerved to miss the girl in time, but that brought them headlong into the path of an oncoming car. She tried to swerve again, but too late, Bianca lost control and they collided.

Bethany was in shock for a few moments, but gradually came to realise what had happened. Their car had been flipped onto its roof and the others were not moving. Bethany struggled with her seat-belt in an attempt to get free, she succeeded and dropped painfully onto the car's roof. She tried to get to her mother; who, like her father and brother, lay suspended upside-down.

"Mum?" Bethany shook her arm as though trying to get her attention. "Mum, wake up!" she sobbed. Her mother was not responding. "Dad?" Neither was her father. They all hung there, silently, motionless. She looked up at her brother; his face was covered with blood. Bethany let out a scream and scrambled to the window by her seat. Seeing someone moving around outside, she banged on the glass. A man bent down to the window, he had a large gash across his

forehead, Bethany could not take her eyes off the mark.

"Are you all right?" the man asked. "I was driving the other car," he looked over to a point that Bethany could not see, and then back to her again. He seemed as disorientated as she was. "I'm sorry," he continued. "Are you hurt?"

"My mum won't wake up!" Bethany cried. "Please help me." She coughed as smoke began to drift around the car.

"Can you open the window?" he asked. "I'll pull you out." Bethany looked around at her family who still hung unconscious from their seats. "Don't worry," the man tried to assure her. "We'll get help for them. Just try to open the window." Bethany pulled at the lever, but it would not budge, she began to thump at the glass.

"It won't open!" she cried.

"Okay..." her companion looked around nervously. "Okay, you stay there, I'll go and get help."

"No, please..."

"It's all right," he said. "I'll be right back and I'll bring help." The man left. As smoke began to billow around her, a panic-stricken Bethany banged loudly on the window.

"Come back!" she screamed. "Please

don't leave me here. Don't leave me!"

Every minute seemed like an hour to Bethany. The man from the other car never came back, but he had called for help and they were there now. Bethany heard a lot of commotion outside the car, but could not understand what people were saying. There was too much noise. Bethany had curled up into a ball and remained that way until she heard a knock at the window. She looked up, and through her tears, she saw a fireman looking back at her.

"Can you hear me?" he asked. Bethany nodded and wiped her eyes. He asked her name, when she first answered he could not make it out, so she shouted it out as though her life depended on it.

"Bethany? That's a pretty name." he said. "I'm Tom."

"Tom." she said quietly. It was inaudible through the glass but Tom understood, he smiled and nodded.

"Are you hurt?" he asked. Bethany was unsure, everything felt numb. She shook her head. Tom explained to her that his colleagues were preparing to cut the car open, they needed to get her brother and parents out and into the waiting ambulances. "Do you understand?" he asked. Bethany

nodded. "Okay," he said. "We'll be as quick as we can." He appeared to nod at someone else outside of Bethany's view.

That was when the noise started. Bethany felt vibrations all around her, she screamed and covered her head with her hands, curling back up into a ball. She heard metal scraping on metal as the car pinged and sparked with the onslaught of machinery cutting into it. Suddenly, the windows shattered, Bethany curled up even tighter to protect herself from the shards of flying glass.

"Hey, hey! Careful!" Tom shouted. Bethany's ears rang at the sudden silence as the machines pulled back before relentlessly gnawing at the car again. Sobbing heavily and choking on the smoke that still surrounded the car, Bethany felt a gloved hand touch her arm. She looked up to see that Tom was still there. She did not take her eyes from his face.

"You okay?" he yelled over the noise. She nodded unable to make any coherent sounds through her coughs and sobs. "Try not to panic," he told her. "It'll all be over soon, I promise." He took her by the hand and she squeezed his tightly, she would hold onto it until she was freed from the wreckage.

* * *

Bethany jolted awake, disturbed by the sound of Brian crashing through the front door. She had dozed off on the sofa and silently cursed herself for doing so. Sitting up groggily, she stared at her uncle as he swayed in the doorway.

"What?!" he slurred. Bethany grimaced, she could smell the alcohol on his breath from across the room.

"Nothing," she replied and stood up. This was going to be one of those times where she would have to fight past him to get to the safety of her room.

"It makes me sick to look at you," Brian sneered.

"Then don't look," she said through gritted teeth.

"You need to learn some resp..." Brian paused and Bethany took a step back, it looked as though he were about to vomit, but he carried on. "You should learn some manners."

Bethany rolled her eyes. "Brian," she groaned, "just go to bed and sleep it off."

Brain said nothing and stood with a hand on either side of the door, blocking the way out. "Get out of my way," she said, her voice becoming more irritable. Brian did not budge. He leaned towards her and looked her up and down, disdainfully.

"I gave up everything because of you," he said.

Bethany shook her head, she had heard him say this before but they had both lost the same things. Whatever it was Brian supposed he had given up, Bethany suspected that it was of his own doing. She had had enough of this and attempted to push past him, but Brian pushed her back. They stood and stared at each other for a while longer, Brian blocking the only escape route and Bethany desperately trying not to show the panic that was beginning to build up inside her.

As Brian lurched forward, Bethany took a few steps back, catching her leg on the coffee table.

"Ow! Shit!" she muttered. Taking off his belt, Brian edged towards her. He had used that belt on Bethany uncountable times since she was twelve years old, she was not prepared to take it this time. "No you don't!" she yelled as Brian lunged forward, swinging the strap of leather. Bethany backed away, it missed her by mere centimetres; she heard it whistle as it swung past her head. Keeping her eyes on Brian, Bethany edged towards the telephone on the table in the corner. Brian came closer, belt lifted high, ready to strike.

There was a knock at the door.

While Brian was momentarily distracted. Bethany saw her chance. Acting on sheer impulse, she grabbed the telephone and swung it as hard as she could, cracking it over Brian's head. She stared at him, he seemed to be looking over her shoulder at nothing, his eyes glazed. Brian swayed and began to topple. Bethany could not tell which way he was going to fall, and before she could move; Brian fell into her, knocking her to the floor.

"Fuck!" She coughed as she landed, having the wind knocked out of her. She tried to push Brian off of her, but she was pinned underneath his weight. She began to panic, for a brief moment she thought he might be dead, but then he grunted – just unconscious. Bethany let out a sharp sound somewhere between a laugh and a cry. Then she heard the door open and someone enter the house.

"Hello?" someone called, "The door was open..." Bethany recognised the voice.

"Kevin!" she yelled.

Appearing in the doorway, Kevin stared, dazed for a second before rushing to her aid and helping to roll Brian onto his side.

“Shit, Bethany,” he said, “what happened?!”

“I thought I'd killed him...” she replied with little more than a whisper. Kevin helped her up from the floor.

“Are you hurt?” he asked.

“No, I don't think so.” Bethany checked herself over vaguely.

“Come on,” said Kevin. “Let's get out of here.”

“Do you think he'll be all right?” Bethany said, looking down at her uncle.

“Fuck him!” Kevin tugged at her arm. “Let's go.”

“I don't understand why you won't go to the police.” Amanda said as she looked dolefully at Bethany, who was now sat in the Marshall's kitchen.

“Mum, can you just leave it?” Kevin said. Amanda shot her son a scornful glance and turned her attention back to the girl, who hung her head and sat quietly. A mug of tea sat in front of her, which had not been touched and had likely gone stone cold by now.

“Bethany?” Amanda prodded.

“Please, Mrs. Marshall,” she replied, “I

just want to forget about it."

"If you're sure?" Amanda said absently, she exchanged a glance with Kevin. Bethany tried to assure them that it was not as bad as it looked, though neither of them were convinced. Amanda considered calling the police regardless of Bethany's protests; she wondered how long it would be before she was badly hurt – or worse.

Sighing, Amanda picked up the mug that sat in front of Bethany and poured the cold liquid down the sink. She asked her guest if she wanted another, but the girl just shook her head.

Bethany looked up at Kevin, who was leaning against one of the counters. "I'm just glad you came by when you did." she said.

"That reminds me," he replied. Reaching into his pocket, Kevin produced Bethany's mobile and placed it on the table in front of her. "You left this behind this afternoon."

"Oh," she said. "I didn't even realise."

"Then think yourself lucky you're so forgetful." Kevin grinned. Bethany smiled too and thought herself very lucky. If Kevin had had no cause to drop by her house that evening she could have ended up suffocating under Brian's weight. Or he could have come to; more angry and violent than before. It was not something Bethany wanted to ponder, so she absently played with her mobile to distract herself from such thoughts.

“What are you going to do now?” Amanda asked. Bethany shrugged; she had no clue where to go from here. She would have preferred not to think about it at that moment, but Amanda was insistent.

“Don't worry about it,” Kevin told her, “it's sorted.”

They both looked at him suspiciously, and before they could ask him any questions, there was a knock at the door. Reaching over to grab the handle, Kevin pulled it open and Peter stepped into the kitchen.

Bethany glared at Kevin accusingly. “You called Peter?”

Kevin shrugged guiltily.

Peter placed a hand on Bethany's shoulder. “You can't go on like this.”

“I don't want to talk about it.” she pulled away from him and glared down at the table. Exchanging a weary glance with Kevin, Peter crouched down in front of Bethany. She looked away.

“We'll drag you kicking and screaming if we have to...” Peter said. After a moment's pause, Bethany relented and looked at him, willing to at least hear him out. He took hold of her hand and said: “I think you should come and live with me.”

14.
Changes

Making a sweep of the bungalow, they could see that Brian was not around. Bethany thought as much, he often left the house before ten o'clock and rarely returned before nightfall. She and her friends had plenty of time to collect her things, but Bethany wanted it done as quickly as possible. She had already waited too long to leave the place behind. Kevin wondered why they had not thought of it before. Bethany had stayed with Peter often enough – he had a spare room, she needed it; why not make it permanent? Peter had been considering it for a while, and Bethany took less convincing than they thought.

Opening the cupboard in the hallway, Bethany found a backpack and two sports bags that belonged to Brian; she figured he would not miss them. She had also acquired three cardboard boxes, one for each of them to carry. Peter lived only a few streets away and Bethany hoped they could achieve the move in one trip.

As the boys stared into the cluttered mess that was her room, Bethany disappeared into the bathroom and emerged moments later with a box full of toiletries and several bottles of brightly coloured hair dye. She stopped at the doorway to her room.

Peter grinned at her. “And all this time, we thought you were compulsively clean.”

Bethany smirked and raised an eyebrow.

“How much of this stuff are we shifting?” asked Kevin, still staring at the chaos.

“Only the essentials,” she replied, “my clothes, guitar and CDs.”

“All of them?” said Kevin. “You own thousands.”

“Dude, you know I can't live without music.”

Kevin nodded in Peter's direction. “You're moving in with a musician.”

Bethany laughed. “I need more than just classical piano to keep me going!” Then turning to Peter she added: “No offence.”

Putting the box down by the door, Bethany entered her room, opened up one of the sports bags and began to throw clothes into it without bothering to fold them. She looked up at the two boys who still stood by the door. “Come on, lads,” she said, clapping twice “Chop, chop!” Kevin perked his eyebrow, he had no idea where to start. Peter could not help but laugh at the expression on his face.

"You heard the lady," he patted Kevin on the shoulder. "Let's get packing."

After a hard morning's work, the three of them sat in the long grass on The Watch. Kevin rolled a cigarette; his shoulders ached from carrying a heavy bag. "Bethany," he said, "don't ever move house again."

She laughed. "It wasn't that bad."

"That's easy for you to say," Kevin replied. "You hardly carried anything."

"Lies and slander!" she scoffed.

"It's true," said Peter. "You had two big, strong handsome guys to do all the work for you."

"Did I?" Bethany grinned widely at Peter, who laughed. She lay back in the long grass and the boys joined her. Listening to the birdsong and the wind rustling through the trees, Bethany smiled. This was a new beginning. It was strange, the effect moving a few streets away had on her; even now it felt as though that chapter of her life had been many years ago, not just a few hours.

Kevin pointed up towards the sky. "That cloud looks like a poodle," he said.

Bethany sniggered. "Dude, they *all* look

like poodles."

"Are you sure that's just tobacco you're smoking there?" asked Peter.

"Oh, come on," said Kevin. "Don't you guys ever look up at the clouds and see shapes?"

"Yeah," Bethany replied. "There's one over there that's shaped like a cloud!"

They laughed and began to pick shapes out in the sky, each suggestion more ridiculous than the last. Eventually, Bethany pointed out a shape that they all agreed upon, a cloud drifted above them that looked much like an angel. They watched quietly as it floated by, distorting into new shapes as it went.

"Do you guys believe in angels?" Kevin asked after a time. The others did not answer at first, but seemed to be giving the matter some serious thought.

"I don't think so," Peter said at last. "I don't believe in Heaven, or Hell, or any of that shit; but I think there is some kind of afterlife." He wondered what his friends would make of it. After a few moments, Bethany asked him to elaborate. "I don't know," he shrugged. "I think sometimes souls stay behind."

"Like ghosts?" she asked. Peter had begun to wish he had not said anything, though Kevin thought it made sense. It was normal for a small town to have its ghost stories, but Gabriel's Watch had more than its fair share.

"This place is Britain's most haunted," said Kevin. Peter smiled, though he got the impression he was being mocked.

Kevin sat up and flicked away his cigarette butt, immediately lighting another. Bethany joined him while Peter remained laying in the grass.

"Still watching those clouds?" Bethany asked him. He propped himself up on his elbows and regarded her, she had a wide smile on her face and he could not help but return it. It had been a long time since he had seen her smile like that. A moment later, Bethany looked away and watched the street below. The three of them sat in quiet contemplation for some time. They had spent many afternoons over several years sitting on The Watch together, only time would tell how many more they would pass.

Kevin sighed and stubbed out a half-finished cigarette. "I should love you and leave you, guys," he said.

"Going so soon?" Bethany asked.

Kevin nodded. "I have to go and face the music with Sean. I can't put it off for much longer." He stood to leave and Bethany looked up at him and smiled.

“Thanks, Kevin.” She did not just mean for his assistance that day, but for helping her out the night before, for calling Peter. Kevin knew what she meant, but he did not need her thanks, his friends would have done the same for him.

“Any time.” He shrugged. Saying goodbye, Kevin descended the hill and the others watched him until he reached the street below.

“Do you think he'll be okay?” Bethany asked.

“With Sean?” Peter replied.

Bethany shook her head. “In general.” To her, Kevin seemed more subdued than normal, he was usually a placid person but never withdrawn. There were also moments where he had been quick to anger, an unusual characteristic for him. “He's been acting weird lately,” Bethany continued. “He was like this after... Y'know.”

“After Karen died?” Peter sat up and thought about it for a while. “I don't know,” he said. “I think he's still shaken after what happened to Alex.”

Bethany sighed and stared out over the town; maybe he was right. Alex's death had shaken them all up, even opened old wounds. Perhaps it was best not to think about it;

things would go back to normal in time.

Arm in arm, Peter and Bethany sauntered along the path that ran through the church yard towards the promenade. As they walked, something caught Bethany's eye. She stopped and looked back to make sure she was not seeing things. Peter turned around to see what she was staring at; and under the willow where they had last seen her, sat Natalie. She was in the same spot where just a few weeks ago she had lost the love of her life – and by the look of it, her sanity.

"Natalie!" Bethany exclaimed. "What are you doing here? People are worried about you."

"No one's worried about me," she replied, not looking at them, just staring into nothingness. Peter and Bethany glanced at each other, then moved closer to Natalie.

"Where have you been?" Peter asked.

"I've been right here." She looked up at him and frowned as though his question was ridiculous. "I've been waiting for Alex."

Bethany arched an eyebrow. "Okay..."

Natalie began to shiver, unlikely from the cold as she wore a heavy sweater and a jacket. It was probably withdrawal, Bethany thought. Peter felt a chill go through him too, the air had suddenly got colder. Natalie hugged her knees close to her chest and began to rock back and forth. She felt Alex's presence as he embraced her from behind.

"It should have been you instead of me," he whispered in her ear.

"It should have been me instead of him," Natalie repeated.

"Nat, don't think like that..." Bethany could think of nothing else to say as she stared uncomfortably at Natalie, still hugging herself and swaying.

Peter remained silent and stared at the spot where Alex and Natalie sat, embracing each other. Alex looked directly at Peter and grinned, it was almost demonic.

"You should go home, Nat," Bethany prodded.

Natalie ignored her and continued to sway. "We'll be together soon," she said.

"Um..." Bethany tugged at Peter's arm, he took the hint.

"We should get going," he said. "I suggest you do the same, Natalie. Go home." With one final tug on his arm, Peter and Bethany turned to walk away.

"'bye!" Alex called out vehemently. Peter looked back over his shoulder.

“'bye.” Natalie repeated.

Bethany turned to see Natalie sat on the ground, shivering. “Poor thing.”

“Yeah.” Peter agreed, looking back at them one last time before walking away.

Kevin had no clue what he was going to say to Sean. He was sure he would think of something, but whatever he said, Kevin knew that it had to be final. Sean sat and scowled for a while before opening with his usual question.

“Have you sold everything, Marshall?”

“You know I haven't,” Kevin replied. “One last batch and that's it; that's what you said.”

“I thought one more wouldn't hurt.”

“It's always one last favour for you, isn't it, Sean?!” Kevin fumed. “I said I wanted out, and I want out!”

Kevin stood and started to pace about the room. Sean sighed. He was angry that Kevin wanted out, but he had never had any problems the whole time he had worked for him; so he thought the least he could do was let this one drop.

“All right, Kev,” he said. “I won't use you any more, just give me those pills and we'll call it quits.” Sean picked up his Rubik's

Cube and began to fiddle with it. Kevin stopped pacing and cleared his throat.

Sean stopped what he was doing and glared up at him. "What?"

"Beth flushed those pills you gave her."

"What?!"

"Hey, don't you get pissed at me!" Kevin yelled. "You shouldn't have got her involved in the first place!"

Sean leaned back in his chair and glared some more. "I expect to be compensated," he said.

"Fine." Kevin shrugged. "I'll pay you for the drugs if that's what it takes, but then we're done, okay? I won't be in debt to you, Sean."

"We'll see," he said flatly as he began twisting the puzzle cube again.

"No, we won't!" Kevin said, snatching the cube from Sean's hands and lobbing it across the room. Sean stared at the empty space between his hands for a second, and then looked up at Kevin. "You're lucky I don't kick your arse."

"Oh, please!" Kevin scoffed. "You don't scare me. You think you're this hard-arse gangster, but you're nothing. You're a fucking loser!"

"Don't speak to me like that!"

"Why?" Kevin yelled. "What are you

going to do? Send your boys after me? I don't give a shit!" For a moment it appeared that his rant was over with, but before Sean could speak, Kevin lunged forwards, pointing a finger in his face. "And another thing, you can forget about any kind of payment for those pills. It's your fault they're lost; not only did you go back on our deal, but you got Beth involved as well-"

"Ah, yes, the lovely Bethany," Sean said evenly, "what am I to do with her."

Kevin slowly shook his head. "You leave her out of it; this is between you and me." He narrowed his eyes. "You think you can threaten my friends and I'll just fall into line? Fuck off!"

Sean said nothing, he leaned back in his chair as he regarded Kevin. Someone was going to have to pay.

"As far as I'm concerned," Kevin continued, "it's over. I want nothing to do with you. Stay away from my friends, and stay away from me."

"And that's it?" Sean shrugged, apparently finding the whole thing amusing. "You think you can just walk away?"

"Just you watch me." Kevin started for the door and as soon as his back was turned, Sean called out to him.

"I'd watch my back if I were you."

Kevin laughed and turned back around to face him. "Get a life, Sean," he said. "Grow up, get a real job and support your son."

"Now you're telling me how to raise my kid?" Sean spat venomously.

Kevin shrugged. "Is this really the example you want to set?" he asked. "Just sort it out." Without leaving any time for a reply, Kevin stormed out of the flat, leaving Sean to fester in his own rage.

After his confrontation with Sean, Kevin went home and shut himself in his room. He put the radio on low and lay on the bed, looking about the room at the various artworks that were pinned along the walls. Kevin raised his left hand and stared meditatively at the deep scar in his palm. This had become a daily ritual.

"Penny for your thoughts?" he heard the sweet voice say. Karen lay next to him on the bed, propping herself up on her elbow, head resting in her palm. Her long, fair hair cascaded over her shoulder. Kevin smiled at her.

"I was just wondering what to do next," he said. "I know what I have to do, I just don't know how."

"I know how," Karen replied. Kevin raised his eyebrows. "Don't worry," she smiled. "We'll be together soon."

Kevin reached out his left hand, she her right. They clasped hands and lay there for a long time, each content with the thought that everything would soon be as it should.

Peter cut quickly through the car park towards the bus stop; he was on his way to face another tedious night shift and wanted to make the journey as quick and painless as possible. Suddenly, he stopped, aware that he was not alone. Turning to look behind him, Peter noticed a boy, no more than twelve years old, standing in the shadows.

The child was dressed in a T-shirt and shorts, hardly suitable for the bitter autumn nights, yet he did not appear cold. Stepping closer, Peter felt the temperature drop several degrees further. Realising that his face was familiar – yet he could not quite place it - Peter stared at the little boy. There was a jolt of recognition as the boy looked up at him pleadingly and spoke.

"You have to go back home."

* * *

Bethany had finally finished unpacking her belongings and placing them in her new room. She lay back on her bed with an exhausted smile on her face. Kevin was right, she should have done this a long time ago – not necessarily move in with Peter, but she should have got away from Brian's place the minute she left high school and got a job. *Better late than never*, she thought.

There was a knock at the door.

"Did you forget your keys again, Pete?" she muttered to herself, as she got up from the bed and made her way to the front door. As she opened it, Bethany froze as she saw Sean standing there.

He smirked as he looked her up and down. "Hello, Beth."

She tried to close the door, but too late. Sean pushed his way into the flat, shutting the door behind him. They stared at each other for a moment, Bethany took two steps back, Sean took two forward. She darted down the hallway in an attempt to reach the telephone, but like a flash, Sean was on her. Just as her hand touched the receiver, he slammed his hand down on top of hers. His other arm encircled her, pinning her arm to her side and holding her tight.

"I don't think so," he said. Gripping her wrist, Sean pulled her away. She struggled, but he tightened his grasp. "You know why I'm here, don't you Beth?"

"Let go of me!" she yelled, kicking at his legs, but her bare feet had no effect on his shins. Sean had positioned himself between Bethany and the front door, but if she could get free she thought she could make it to the kitchen: grab a knife: defend herself.

She squirmed as he spoke into her ear, keeping his voice low. "You got rid of something that belongs to me," he said. "I'm not very happy, but perhaps you and I can think of a way for you to pay me back."

"Pete will be back in a minute," Bethany said desperately.

"No he won't," Sean replied. "I just saw him leave for work."

This bastard had been watching her; everything seemed hopeless. Silent tears began to roll down her cheeks.

"Now, are you going to be a good girl," Sean continued, "or are you going to make this harder on yourself?"

"Fuck you!" Bethany had no intention of making it easy for either of them. If he wanted to kick and punch her, break her bones, she could handle that, but not this. He started to drag her down the hallway, towards the bedroom.

"No!" She screamed. Kicking wildly, she attempted to thrust her elbow into Sean's stomach, but he was too strong. He grasped her so tightly around the waist that it knocked the wind out of her.

He laughed as she whimpered and still attempted to wriggle free. "Go on, struggle," he said. "I like a challenge."

"Get off of her!" Peter's voice. A wave of relief rushed over Bethany. Sean released his hold on her and she almost dropped to the floor. Both turned to face Peter, who now stood in the doorway. Bethany backed away from her assailant, steadying herself against the wall.

"Are you okay, Beth?" Peter asked her, his eyes focused on Sean. Taking a few seconds to calm herself down, she eventually managed to answer.

"I'm okay."

Still glaring at Sean, Peter snarled, "Get out."

Sneering at Bethany, Sean pushed past Peter and left, slamming the door behind him. Peter turned his attention to his friend.

"Are you sure you're okay?" he asked.

Bethany nodded. She was clearly shaken but appeared to be unharmed. "Okay," said Peter. "Wait here." With that, he exited after Sean.

Peter caught up with him outside. Grabbing Sean by the shoulder, Peter threw him against the wall.

"All right Pete?" Sean grinned, "There's no need for violence." He seemed amused by the situation, Peter was not. He placed his hands on the wall on either side of Sean.

"Listen to me, you piece of shit..."

"I'd be careful if I were you," Sean sneered.

"What?" Peter scoffed. "You'll send some of your mates after me, is that it?" He had heard all these empty threats before. "You're not the only one who has friends."

Sean grunted and attempted to push away, but Peter pushed his forearm up under Sean's chin, pinning him back by his throat. Sean coughed and the colour drained from his face as he squirmed like a bug.

"You think people fear you," Peter continued, "but they don't. You're just a pathetic cunt who gets his kicks from those who are weaker than him."

Sean clawed at Peter's arm, trying to get free, but he was stuck there.

"What kind of person threatens a girl half

his size?" Peter said. "Now, let's get one thing straight, if you touch her again, your life won't be worth living." He relinquished his hold on Sean and placed his hands back on the wall, ready to thwart any attempts to get away.

Sean coughed and clutched at his throat. "I won't go near her again. Okay?"

Peter glared at him; he was not prepared to take Sean at his word.

"No," Peter reiterated, "you won't go near her again, and you can stay away from Kevin, and most of all, stay out of my way."

In the shadows, Peter noticed a frail looking, dark-haired woman watching them. What was it with the shadows this evening? Again, this woman was familiar; Peter had spoken to her before. Looking back at Sean, he continued his verbal onslaught.

"You're nothing more than a self-centred, sadistic bigot, you know that? Always looking out for number one."

"Everyone does," Sean protested.

"No." Peter shook his head. He noticed the woman had moved closer. "Let's talk about the mother of your child."

Sean went white. "What?" he said, almost inaudibly.

"You heard," said Peter. "The woman, who

you lead people to believe, had ran off and left you with a baby." He watched as Sean went whiter still. "But that's not what happened, is it?" Peter continued. "You were making easy money, selling the drugs that killed her. You couldn't have people think the stuff you sold was bad, could you?"

"No one knew about that," Sean whispered.

"As I said," Peter replied, "you're not the only one with friends." He glanced at the woman now standing next to them and smirked. "How do you think she'd feel," he asked, "knowing that you were raising her son that way?"

The woman glared at Sean, not that he could see her. Though he looked shaken now, Peter wondered if he would ever change.

1999

Sean entered his girlfriend's flat, he could hear the baby crying.

"Nicole?" he called. No answer. He hoped that she had not gone out and left the baby on his own; or even worse, that she was getting high. That infuriated Sean – that she would continue taking drugs, even with a

baby to look after.

"Nicole?" He opened the door to the living room, which was unoccupied. On the coffee table, Sean noticed the remnants of what was once Nicole's stash. Surely she had not taken all that already?

Sean sighed heavily and made for the bedroom, where the baby still cried. On first opening the door, Sean looked towards his son laying in his cot; but his eyes soon moved to the heap on the floor, Nicole's body. Her frail figure lay contorted, her long, dark her scattered around her, a few strands covering her face. Her skin was blue and her eyes wide open, staring blankly up at Sean. He winced.

Walking over to the cot, Sean picked up his son. "Hey Jack, it's all right," he said. The baby stopped crying. "Let's take you home." Sean took one last look at the body on the floor before he left.

Peter walked into the living room, where Bethany was sat on the sofa. She rubbed her wrist, which was beginning to bruise where Sean had gripped it so relentlessly.

Peter sat down next to her. "You okay?" he asked. She stared at him blankly for a moment.

"You didn't hurt him, did you?" she prodded. Bethany thought back to a time in high school when Peter had lost his temper with Sean, laid into him and broke his nose. She hoped he had done it again.

"No, of course not," Peter replied, his lips curving in a devious smirk.

Bethany returned the smile then shrugged. "Shouldn't you be getting to work?"

"I'll call in sick," he replied. Bethany stared at him. "Don't worry," Peter said, putting his arm around her. "Sean's a reasonable man, he won't bother you again."

Bethany perked an eyebrow and looked at Peter suspiciously. "What did you say to him?"

"Nothing," he replied. Bethany sighed and rested her head on his shoulder. She realised it was probably for the best that she did not know.

15.
Regret

Bethany lay on her bed, unable to sleep. This was the third night in a row. She stared at her surroundings and listened to the clock ticking, it sounded louder than usual. She heard mumbling from the next room, Peter was talking in his sleep again.

Shutting her eyes, Bethany tried to will herself to sleep; it was a tactic that never worked. It was almost two o'clock in the morning. Peter's ramblings were becoming progressively louder. *What a great match for flatmates*, Bethany thought, *a sleep-talker and an insomniac.*

She glared at the clock as it seemed to deliberately tick louder. Peter's subconscious murmurings were becoming more coherent, she could now make out full sentences. Not that she cared; that was not what was disturbing her. She looked over to the books on the shelf, if she was going to be awake she may as well read.

Bethany reached for one of the books, then paused. She thought she heard Peter call her name. Sitting up, she listened harder.

"Bethany!"

She definitely heard it that time and wondered if Peter was still talking in his sleep or had actually called her. Getting out of bed, Bethany opened the door and stepped into the hallway. Despite trying to go quietly, the floorboards creaked beneath her feet as she made her way towards Peter's room.

Bethany stood by the door and listened. After a few seconds of silence, she heard him mutter something. Knocking lightly, Bethany hesitated for a moment before pushing the door open.

"Peter?" There was no answer, but an eerie chill suddenly caught her. Shivering, she threw the feeling off and walked over to where he lay. "Pete," she whispered. Bethany made to shake him awake, but he rolled over and started to talk again.

"We love you," he said. "We all do, and we miss you."

Bethany stepped back and frowned. "Pete," she said a little louder.

"Don't feel guilty," he continued. "Live your life and be happy..." he trailed off and turned over again. "Please," he said, "just leave her alone."

Bethany rolled her eyes, stepped forward and grabbed Peter sharply by the shoulder. "Wake up!" She shook Peter again and he jerked awake, she jumped back.

"Beth... what the fuck...?" Peter blearily groped for the lamp by his bed.

Looking down at her feet, Bethany shrugged. "Sorry," she said. "I didn't know whether I should wake you."

Peter frowned and stared at her bemusedly.

"You were talking random bollocks in your sleep again," she explained as she perched on the edge of the bed. Peter watched her for a moment and guessed that there was more to it than that.

"What's bothering you?"

Bethany shrugged; she wished she knew. He held his arm out to offer her a hug, she clambered over to him. Pulling the covers over her, Peter squeezed her tight. "Things get better in their own, in time," he said. "Try to get some sleep."

Bethany lay her head on Peter's chest and listened to the rhythm of his heart beating. He began to play with the hair at the nape of her neck, Bethany sighed and shut her eyes."I love you, Pete," she said. "You're my best friend."

Peter kissed the top of her head. "I love you too, Beth." Though she did not hear him; she had already drifted off to sleep.

* * *

Smoke slowly began to fill the car. Bethany looked around; the others were motionless. Everything was still except for the sound of footsteps outside. Bethany banged on the window and peered outside. She saw the feet belonging to the person outside stop in front of the window. He stooped down. Brian.

She scrambled away from the window, smoke surrounded her. No escape. Brian knocked on the glass.

"Bethany," he beckoned. "Give me your hand and I'll pull you out."

The smoke was becoming too think to breathe. There was no other way out; it was Brian or death.

"Beth..." Her uncle reached his hand out towards her as though the glass was not there. "Beth..."

"Beth!"

Opening her eyes, the first thing that Bethany saw was her parents and brother standing at the foot of the bed. She squeezed her eyes shut, when she opened them again they were gone - just an hallucination, an echo from the dream.

"Beth, what's wrong?"

She looked up, bleary eyed, still lying in

Peter's arms.

"I had a bad dream," she said, burying her head in his shoulder.

"It's over now," he said.

Bethany hugged him tighter. "I saw my parents," she continued, "and the crash, Brian was there..."

"It was only a dream," Peter assured her. They always seemed so real to her, though; it took her a few minutes to calm down, to realise where she was, to realise she was safe.

She looked up at Peter and a strand of greenish-blue hair fell in front of her face. He swept the strand away, tucking it behind her ear. He left his hand cupping her face; they stared at each other for some time.

There was a slow, mutual realisation of what they wanted, though they both held back, each unsure of the other's reciprocation. It was Bethany who made the first move. She tilted her head, it was all the invitation Peter needed – they kissed.

Bethany allowed herself that moment of weakness, but there was a niggling voice in the back of her mind which she chose to ignore.

Pulling her closer, Peter kissed her deeply. Bethany's back arched as he slowly ran his hand down her spine, as his caresses reached the small of her back, Bethany listened to that little voice in her head. She pushed him away.

"Don't," she said. "I'm sorry, I can't do this."

"Why?" Peter's voice momentarily betrayed his disappointment. Bethany avoided his gaze, she seemed flushed.

"It's okay," he said. "Whatever it is, you can tell me. I won't be offended."

She looked up at him uncomfortably; uncertain of what to say. Peter wondered if she felt pressured, or that it was all too weird. It seemed that they would be nothing more than friends, and he had to be content with that.

Bethany cleared her throat. "It's not that I don't want to..." she said at last.

Peter said nothing, allowing her to continue in her own time. Bethany sighed, there was a part of herself that she did not care to show to anyone; a part that left her feeling ashamed through no fault of her own. If she showed that part to Peter he would realise the extent of her humiliation and she was not sure if that was something she could bear. She sat up rigidly and Peter propped himself up on his elbow and watched her intently. Bethany looked down at him, she wished he would not look so concerned, that made things worse. She knew that she could trust him, but opening up was not easy; she owed it to both of them to at least try.

"You know I've never been with a guy before..." she said.

"You're a virgin?" Peter raised his eyebrows.

In spite of herself Bethany laughed. "Why sound so surprised?" she said. "I've never even had a boyfriend."

Peter had not actually thought about it, but now it made sense. "That's okay," he said. Sitting up, he rubbed her back, Bethany flinched.

"That's not it," she said. Peter looked confused; Bethany sighed and tried to explain as best she could. "I could never let myself get close to anyone..."

She could not think of what else to say, there were no words to describe how she felt, torn between Peter and her own self-loathing. She looked at him and he sat up next to her, putting an arm around her shoulder. Bethany shut her eyes briefly, why did he have to be so good to her? Sighing, she rested her forehead against his; she felt safe here, she still wanted him. She could not tell him what was wrong, but he would see for himself soon enough.

Kissing him tentatively, Bethany hoped that Peter had not changed his mind. He responded tenderly and she allowed herself to be lead. As he pulled her T-shirt over her head, Bethany seemed to shrink as Peter saw for the first time the extent of Brian's abuse. No wonder she had initially recoiled from his touch, she must have been in constant pain.

Bethany turned her head to avoid catching sight of Peter's expression. This was the side of herself that she had never shown to anyone, she felt more vulnerable now than she ever had; and no matter how bad it looked on the outside, inside she felt so much worse. The bruises all but covered her back and sides, and they were laced with welt marks, some were still fresh, others had left scars.

Peter was silent; he had not known that things had become that bad. He gently stroked the small of her back where most of the bruising gathered, being gentle now he knew she was sore. He only ever wanted to protect her, but this was something entirely out of his control.

"I must look hideous," Bethany whispered, her eyes lowered involuntarily.

Peter tried to suppress a small laugh. "No you don't." He took Bethany by the chin and turned her face to his. “You're beautiful.”

Bethany stared at him; she looked as though she were on the verge of crying, though she shed no tears. “I don't want to hurt any more.”

Peter kissed her on the forehead then held her close; it was all he could do. As much as he wanted to he could not take her pain away.

“No one's going to hurt you again.” Peter felt that was a stupid thing to say as soon as he heard himself say it; an empty promise, but it was all he could offer her.

Bethany leaned in to kiss him again. “Just take it slowly, okay?”

Peter had not expected her to want to continue, but Bethany had nothing more to hold back. They shared themselves with each other that night and for the first time in weeks, Bethany slept soundly, with Peter's arms around her. Waking the next morning, Peter reached out to find an empty bed; Bethany had gone.

“Bethany?” Kevin raised his eyebrows and grinned. “You and Bethany?”

“I'm glad you find it amusing.” Peter replied bitterly. He was beginning to wish he had not said anything. Bethany had not gone to work after leaving the flat that morning, nor was she answering Peter's calls. He was worried about her and thought maybe Kevin had seen her, so now he sat in the Marshall's kitchen drinking coffee and listening to Kevin's commentary on the situation.

"So, are you two an item now?" Kevin grinned.

Peter absent-mindedly played with his coffee mug and looked up at Kevin, clearly unimpressed. "Not exactly," he said flatly. "If this morning is anything to go by, I doubt she's interested."

"Ouch." Kevin replied, lighting a cigarette he had been rolling.

"I think I made a mistake." Peter said.

Kevin shrugged. "Not much you can do about it now."

Peter leaned back in his chair and sighed. It was times like this when he wondered if his friend was being deliberately unhelpful. "This is Beth we're talking about," Kevin continued. "She'll turn up eventually."

Peter finally cracked a smiled. "You make her sound like a stray cat."

"You guys will sort it out," Kevin laughed. "You always do."

Peter's mobile rang. He quickly fished it from his pocket, hoping that it was Bethany, but looking at the number, it was not one of his contacts. He answered it.

As Kevin watched him, he saw the expression on Peter's face drop. “What is it?” he asked. Peter looked at him but did not answer, he listened quietly to the person on the other end of the line. After ending the call, Peter stared at Kevin.

“I have to go,” he said.

“What's happened?” Kevin asked.

“It's Beth,” Peter replied. “She's just been taken into hospital.”

Bethany made her way up The Watch in search of solitude. She walked along the promenade, through the gates into the church yard and headed through the thick undergrowth towards the back of the church. As she walked, Bethany heard the crunch of fallen leaves just behind her, followed by a familiar voice calling her name.

It was Natalie. Bethany was glad to see her; despite coming up here to be alone, deep down she desperately wanted company, and any company would do.

“Nat!” she exclaimed, seeing that she was dressed that same as the last time she saw her. The clothes were filthy and tattered. “What are you still doing up here?"

Natalie shrugged and leaned against a decrepit headstone. "I can't leave," she said, "not yet."

Bethany considered saying something regarding the woman's state of mind, but she thought better of it.

"Mind if I join you?" she asked.

"Please do." Natalie grinned.

They sat down in the shade of a willow tree with their backs leaning against a tombstone. Bethany reached into her jacket pocket, pulled out a bottle of vodka and took a swig from it.

"It's a bit early in the day, isn't it?" Natalie remarked. Bethany said nothing and offered the bottle to her. She readily accepted it and after taking a couple of gulps, handed it back. Natalie studied her for a few moments. "What brings you up here?" she asked.

"I've made a mistake," Bethany replied, "and I'd like to forget about it."

"Just hiding out 'til it all blows over, huh?" said Natalie.

Bethany laughed. "Something like that."

"This mistake," Natalie asked, "can it be amended?"

Bethany shrugged. "I guess so."

"Because not everything can be put right."

Natalie added.

Bethany was not sure which one of them she was referring to, either way it made her feel uneasy. She was not sure how big a mistake she had made and she had been too much of a coward to stay to find out, and that had very likely aggravated the situation. Bethany drank a little more from the vodka bottle and handed it back.

"I wish I could fix all my mistakes." Natalie said as she passed the bottle back.

"What mistakes?" Bethany asked.

"Take your pick!" she replied. "All the shit I've put my parents through, all the friends I've lost over the years – and I know it's all my own doing. Then of course, there's Alex." Natalie paused for breath and stared dimly into the distance. "He's dead because of me."

"Nat," said Bethany. "You can't keep doing this to yourself."

"Why shouldn't I?" she said bitterly. "It's the truth."

Natalie had been a constant source of worry and misery to anyone who cared about her. Most of her family had given up on her, as had all of her friends, except for Alex. He had tried to help her but she pushed him – at first she pushed him away, then when he refused to go, she pushed him to try what she was taking. Just one time, then another, and another. After a while, she did not have to push him at all.

"I think it would be best for everyone if I were dead." Natalie said.

Bethany's eyes widened. "Oh my God! Natalie, is that what you meant by joining Alex?" She shook her head. "That's not the answer."

"I don't want to die," Natalie replied, "but you know it's your time to go when you see people you care about, the ones who are no longer with you."

Bethany shuddered and continued to drink from the bottle. "Sometimes I think I see things," she said, "and they seen so real..."

"I'm not seeing things." Natalie protested. "I see Alex as clear as I see you." She fumbled around inside her jacket pocket and pulled out a bottle of pills. She shook it and the tablets rattled around inside. "I keep thinking about it," she said, "what it would be like. I haven't had the guts to do it yet."

Bethany regarded her for a moment. "It takes more guts not to do it." She had a feeling that Natalie was no longer listening. It appeared to Bethany that she was not going to get any kind of response from her, but she carried on regardless. "What happened to

Alex wasn't your fault. He chose to do heroin, you didn't force him."

Natalie laughed bitterly. "Yes, I did."

"He could have said no" said Bethany. "He wouldn't blame you for this."

"He would." Natalie stared vacantly into the trees.

Bethany sighed and stared at the ground. She began to feel nauseated, perhaps she had drunk too much. She drank some more. "Sometimes I feel that I should have died with my family." Bethany said, hoping that Natalie might start to see sense and open up to her. She looked at Bethany and nodded, she knew exactly what she meant.

"They won't leave you alone until they get what they want," she said.

Bethany looked at her and frowned. "Okay, Nat... You're scaring me now."

Natalie started to rock back and forth with her knees pulled up to her chest. The two were shivering; the temperature had plummeted. As Bethany gulped back more of the booze, she noticed that someone else was with them. She stared, her vision beginning to blur. A boy, no more than twelve years old, stood staring at her. His attire was fit for summer, he must have been freezing, but he did not appear to be cold.

Bethany looked away from the boy and saw that Natalie was grinning at her inanely. Her head was tilted to the side and rested on her knees. "Who do you see, Beth?"

Staring at the boy, Bethany knew who he was though she could not bring herself to believe it. "John...?" she whispered. The boy stepped back as though surprised that she acknowledged him. He turned to walk away and Bethany stood to follow him. She stumbled and had to grab hold of the nearest tree branch to steady herself. She felt sick in the pit of her stomach and her head was spinning.

Natalie stood to help steady her. "Beth, take it easy."

"Where did he go?" Bethany staggered forward, unsteady on her feet. Natalie followed her, prepared to catch her if she stumbled again

"I don't see anything." Natalie said, looking about her.

"He was right there..." Bethany pointed to a spot in front of her. She faltered, clutching her stomach as she doubled up in pain. Natalie put her hand on her shoulder and Bethany looked up at her with a glazed expression, trying to focus. "I don't feel so good..." Bethany turned away, collapsed to her knees and vomited.

"Better?" asked Natalie.

Bethany nodded groggily, getting to her feet; she saw him again. John was standing there, amongst the trees, but this time there were two other people with him. Two people who Bethany recognised instantly. "Mum and dad..." she whispered.

"What?" Natalie looked confused, even concerned. She shook Bethany by the arm.

"I have to go." Looking around nervously, Bethany pushed through the thicket back towards the pathway. Natalie called after her and followed.

They walked across to the promenade where the stone statue of Gabriel stood. Bethany paused for a moment at the head of the stone stairway and looked down it. She swayed and grabbed hold of the hand rail. Natalie stood right behind her. "Beth, what happened?"

She shakily turned to face Natalie. From within the church yard, Bethany could still see her family, watching her. Bethany shut her eyes and shook her head. "It's nothing," she said. "I feel sick and I just want to go home." Bethany moved away from the steps and leaned against the balustrade, she had begun to feel dizzy.

"Are you okay?" Natalie asked, but Bethany did not hear her. Her legs gave way and she fell. Bethany heard the sound of something crack as she hit the ground, then everything went black.

The fluorescent lights stung her eyes. Bethany groaned as she tried to raise her head, the movement nauseated her so she stayed still. Slowly becoming accustomed to the brightness around her, she opened her eyes but had to close them again as the room began to spin. Vaguely aware of a soft murmuring voice, she tried to focus on it.

"...look at me...keep your eyes open...it's okay..."

Bethany squinted and lifted her head to see the kind face of a woman staring back at her. *A nurse. Fantastic.* Bethany hated hospitals, she had to get out of there. Fighting to keep her eyes open, she stared at the woman in front of her.

"Can you tell me your name?" the nurse asked, holding her hand. As Bethany tried to sit up, pain shot through her left arm. She cried out a fell back onto the bed.

"Tell me what hurts."

"Everything." Bethany began to cry and

the nurse gently squeezed her shoulder.

Turning away from the woman's sympathetic gaze, Bethany looked around, taking in her surroundings. She was in a small cubicle. Through the open curtain she saw a busy department – from the amount of people and noise, she guessed she was in Accident and Emergency. It had been a long time since Bethany had been in a place like this, not since -

She froze when she saw them. As real as they had seemed to her on The Watch, her family stood watching her. *You know it's your time to go when you see the ones who are no longer with you...* Was Natalie right? Had her family come for her? She was not ready to die.

"I won't go with you." Bethany glared at her family and yelled with more conviction. "I'm not going anywhere with you!"

They looked sad, dejected. Good. Bethany turned away and looked up at the nurse's puzzled frown.

"You need to tell us if you've taken something."

Bethany stared at the wall and made no answer.

"Tell me what you've taken." The nurse placed a gentle hand on the girl's shoulder.

“Nothing.” She looked back over her shoulder and saw that her family was still there. “Just leave me alone!” Bethany rolled onto her side and was caught between screams and hysterical sobs as the nauseating pain shot through her arm once more. Pain was good, it meant she was alive. She clung to it.

After much searching and endless enquiries, Peter finally found his way onto the ward. There was one nurse sat at the desk, she looked up at him, seemingly annoyed at being disturbed. Peter asked where he could find Bethany and the nurse regarded him for a moment. “You're not a relative, are you?” she asked, flatly.

“I'm her flatmate, and her next of kin.” That counted for more than any relative Bethany had. “How is she?”

The nurse huffed and looked at her files, it seemed to Peter that she resented having to do any work. She told him that Bethany had a fractured wrist and seemed to be hallucinating when she was admitted.

“It doesn't look like she's taken anything, but she has drunk almost a whole bottle of vodka,” the nurse concluded, “she's sleeping it off now."

Peter took a step back. Why would she do that?

"Can I see her?" he asked.

"Visiting hours are six 'til eight."

Peter had spent many hours looking for Bethany and he was not going to leave now. The nurse looked up at him, scowling. She saw that he had no intention of going anywhere and she could not be bothered to argue. She huffed and pointed towards a ward room further along the hall.

"Five minutes; no more."

There where four beds in the room, though three were empty. In the fourth bed, Bethany lay on her side staring vacantly ahead. Her heart sank when Peter walked into the room, he was the one person who could make her feel worse than she already did. She watched him as he walked towards her, but she said nothing.

Peter reached out to touch her but she jerked away from him, her eyes fixed on his.

"Don't," she warned.

Peter sighed and pulled his hand away. He slumped into the chair next to the bed.

"What the hell happened to you?" he asked.

Bethany shrugged, wincing at the pain still

nagging in her wrist. Carefully, she shuffled into a seated position and stared silently at her friend. At first Peter thought that she was not going to talk to him, but eventually she said, "I fucking hate hospitals."

"I know." Peter put his hand gently on Bethany's shoulder, but she pulled away from him again. He wondered whether it was because she was sore or because he repulsed her. It was hard to tell by the way she stared at him him; expressionless.

A few moments went by while neither of them said anything. Peter wondered how his friend had become so self-destructive; what was going through her mind? He had to know. "The nurse said you downed a bottle of vodka..."

"I don't want to talk about it." From the tone of her voice, Peter knew that she was not just referring to the alcohol. He also noticed the slightest flicker of defiance in her eyes. It seemed his friend was still there, even if subdued.

"Beth, what's wrong with you?"

She looked away and began to bite her thumbnail.

"You didn't take anything, did you?"

"No!" She glared at him. "Of course I fucking didn't!"

Peter felt ashamed that he had even suggested it. She had smoked a little weed but never anything else, he knew that; he just needed to hear it from her.

"The nurse said you were seeing things." Peter inched the chair closer to the bed. He looked Bethany in the eye, but she turned her face away, staring instead at the foot of the bed. She began to shake. Was it from the cold, or fear? Perhaps both.

"Beth," Peter leaned in closer to her. "Tell me what you see."

She continued to stare at the same spot and shook her head adamantly. "I can't," she whispered. He followed her gaze to the foot of the bed where Bethany's family stood. They stared back at him; the woman spoke.

"Please."

"What do you see?" Peter asked again.

"I think they've come back for me," Bethany's voice trembled quietly. "My family - I should have died with them."

Peter frowned. "Why would you think that? That's not why they're here."

She slowly turned her head to face him. Her expression was somewhere between confusion and suspicion. He had already said too much, he may as well continue. As Bethany's family looked on expectantly, Peter sighed and resigned himself to the truth.

"It's really important that you listen to me." He took hold of her hand and she did not pull away this time. She stared at him, nonplussed. "I mean it," he continued, "if you've ever trusted me with anything, I need you to trust me with this."

"I don't understand..." Bethany's brow furrowed deeper and Peter squeezed her hand tightly in both of his.

"It's okay," he said. "I see them too. And I can talk to them. They've asked me to speak to you."

"How?" Surely she and Peter could not be sharing the same delusion? She remembered him hinting about ghosts on numerous occasions, but she had never thought to take it seriously.

"Ever since I was a kid," Peter said, "they would talk to me, I don't just mean your parents, but... others?" he tried to think of the right words but could not. He shrugged and continued. "But that's not important right now." He was not sure whether she believed him, but she made no answer, just stared blankly at him.

"Sometimes souls stay behind," Peter continued, "if there is sadness, or something left undone or when someone can't let go."

He watched as a single tear rolled down her cheek, Peter squeezed her hand harder. “You have to let go, Bethany.”

Letting out a small cry, Bethany's shoulders heaved as the tears began to flow. “I never got to say goodbye,” she said. “I never got to tell them them that I love them.”

“They know,” said Peter. “They love you too.” He looked back towards the family that stood at the end of the bed, they smiled, grateful that their message was finally getting through. “They say they don't blame you, they never did. Most importantly,” Peter added, “you have got to stop blaming yourself.”

“Is that why they're still here,” Bethany spoke in between sobs. “Because of me?” She had spent so many years going through the incident in her head and could not help but wonder if her family would still be there if she had not been fighting with John. In their last few moments together they had all been shouting at each other, and that had been bad enough; now it seemed her family were left behind because of her tendency to torment herself.

“They just want to see you safe and happy,” Peter said, “and they just want to say goodbye.” Peter briefly looked back at

Bethany's family before delivering the last of their message. “They're sorry for everything you went through, but they're proud of the person you've become and they'll always love you – even John.”

Bethany managed to let out a little laugh through her sobs. She was unsure what to make of the experience but she knew Peter was right; she could not go on blaming herself. She felt she could now be released from her self-imposed sentence.

She watched as her family faded from her vision, knowing it would be the last time she saw them. With a mixture of sadness, joy, but mostly relief, she let them go. After moment, she looked up at Peter and asked: “Why did you never tell me this before?”

He shrugged. “To be honest I'm just getting used to it myself.”

Bethany said nothing, they sat in awkward silence for a moment. Peter watched her as she avoided his gaze once again, he wondered if he had done something wrong, it was hard to tell lately. He needed to know what was going on in her head, whether she wanted to talk about it or not.

“Beth...” Peter was startled by a banging on the window, he looked over his shoulder to see the nurse standing there, pointing at her watch. Peter sighed as he and Bethany looked at each other.

"Look, I have to go," he said. Bethany just nodded her response. "They said they're going to keep you in overnight," he continued. "I'll pack you a bag and bring it back later."

"Okay," Bethany said quietly. Peter sighed heavily; she seemed to have reverted to her unresponsive self. He told himself that it was probably just the shock, and hoped that she would be less taciturn later.

As Bethany watched him leave, a new kind of guilt began to well up inside. She wished she had not been so cold, but she found it hard to communicate. Everything seemed so surreal. Everything was different.

16.
Letting Go

Peter had wanted to share his secret with Bethany for a long time. He could have only ever imagined her reaction – she might not believe him, think he was lying or delusional, maybe even be scared of him. Peter had never thought the outcome would be positive, so he had kept quiet, fearing her response.

Circumstances had changed, he had been faced with a dilemma; risk his friendship with Bethany - which was already wearing thin - by telling her the truth, or keep withholding his secret, allowing her to continue on her path of self-destruction. In the end there was no choice, Bethany's well-being meant more to him than anything else. How they would carry on from that point, he did not know.

Shutting the front door, Peter walked down the hallway and chucked his keys onto the telephone table. The answering machine's light was flashing, he pushed the button and the machine bleeped into action. Peter listened as a drunken Natalie chattered excitedly, "Hey, Pete, um... Beth's had an accident – nothing serious – but she's been taken in to hospital. I thought I should let you know, because I can't go with her."

Thanks for nothing, Peter thought as Natalie continued: "She's gone to Saint Michael's... I've got to go..." She seemed to be talking to someone else. "What?... No, Alex, I'm not going anywhere!"

The line went dead. Peter rolled his eyes and muttered "Twat" under his breath as he erased the message. He would have to find Natalie later. Right now he had more important things to deal with, and as Natalie said herself, she was not going anywhere.

Peter headed for his room and the moment that he set foot inside he could tell that something was not quite right. Looking around he noticed that the window was wide open, Peter was sure that he had only left it ajar. He pushed the window closed, nausea crawling through him at the thought of someone going through his things.

Then the notion hit him that there might still be someone there. A quick search of the flat eased his fears. There was no one else there now, and there did not appear to be anything missing. Yet there was the nagging feeling that something was amiss. Searching frantically through drawers and cupboards, Peter still found nothing to be lost. He paused for a moment, sitting down on his bed. Almost instantly, the answer hit him.

Leaping off the bed, Peter searched under the mattress, but he could not find what he was looking for. He pulled the mattress up and pushed it clear off the bed – nothing. He looked underneath the bed, but the gun was gone.

"Shit!"

The nausea returned.

No one could have known that Peter had hidden it there, he had not told anyone, not even Bethany. Now it was clear that someone else had hold of it, but who? Peter cursed under his breath as he pulled his bed back together, then he sat down upon it, head in hands. Now what?

1989

Philip threw the door open and ushered his family in from the rain. They had been caught in the downpour for less than a minute, but they were already soaked through. They laughed breathlessly as they dripped puddles onto the floor in the hallway.

Imogen leaned on the table for support, rubbing her aching back. Pregnancy was uncomfortable enough without having to make mad dashes through the rain. She had three more months of it to endure; if she had remembered it being so bad the first time, she would have stopped at one child.

Philip tried to make a fuss over her, but she waved him away, grimacing as she peeled her wet coat off. She watched Peter as he wrestled with his scarf, he always knotted it in such a way that he could not get it off again - just like his father. Imogen rolled her eyes and helped him out of his scarf before he strangled himself.

"Get that coat off, sweetheart," she added, "or you'll catch a dea-" Imogen stood upright and locked eyes with her husband. "What was that?" she whispered.

They stood silently, listening. There it was again; a light clattering from somewhere in the house. They looked down the hallway towards the kitchen where the sound came from.

Peter stood frozen to the spot as Imogen's arms encircled him defensively. Philip crept towards the kitchen, pushing the door ajar. Through the crack they could see the stranger brazenly rifling through their belongings, drawers and cupboard doors left open, much of the contents strewn across the floor. The man continued his search, oblivious to their presence.

They had to call the police. The cordless telephone sat on the kitchen counter, which meant confronting their uninvited guest. Philip turned to his wife and motioned for her to stay where she was. Imogen pulled Peter further back into the hallway and crouched down in front of him.

"Stay out of sight, y'understand?"

Peter nodded and sat on the bottom step, peeking through the bannisters as his mother grabbed her bag from the hall table and returned to her husband's side. A long time seemed to pass before Philip made his move.

The intruder started as the door banged open. He stood frozen, watching the couple staring back at him.

"What the fuck are you doing in my house?!" Philip demanded.

The intruder threw his hands up and laughed nervously. He was agitated, delirious, unstable. It was likely he could be dangerous. Philip mimicked the man's posture though his arms were out in a calming gesture rather than defensive. The man's agitation seemed to ease in response.

Imogen placed her bag on the side and slowly reached for the telephone.

"Don't even think about it!" The intruder pulled a gun from his jacket. His hand shook violently as he pointed it at her. Imogen stepped away from the receiver and casts a glance towards Peter, still sat on the stairs, his eyes wide and face frozen in horror as he looked on.

Philip placed himself between his wife and the gun wielding maniac.

"You'd shoot a pregnant woman?"

The intruder's lip curled in a grimacing smirk. "I need money, jewellery, whatever you've got," he said. "Just hand it over, no one needs to get hurt."

He was desperate, a frightened creature backed into a corner. He did not want to squeeze the trigger, but his agitated state meant he was likely to lash out if he felt threatened.

"Just calm down," Imogen told him as she reached into her bag. The intruder eyed her nervously as she blindly searched the contents of her bag, watching him the whole time. She was going to throw him her wallet, the intruder thought, then he could get out of there before they called the police.

"Imogen, what are you doing?"

She ignored her husband, and then she found what she was looking for. She took a deep breath, counting to three in her head.

"Drop it!" she yelled as she whipped the pistol from her bag and aimed it at the man's head.

"Imogen! What the fuck...?" Philip spat. "Why do you have that thing!?"

"Protection," she replied flatly. "I didn't move to this country so my family could be threatened like this." She did not take her eyes from the stranger. She spoke slowly. "I said, put the gun down."

Though highly strung, the intruder appeared to comply. He loosened his grip on his gun, placing his palms out as though surrendering. Imogen lowered her own weapon, but too soon. The man lunged forward, knocking the gun from her hand sending it skidding across the floor. He pointed his weapon at the woman's chest. She gasped and backed into the counter. Philip grabbed hold of the man's wrist, pointing the gun away from his wife.

Out in the hallway, Peter looked on. He could do something, he could run and grab the telephone, call the police, but he stayed rooted to the spot; unable to move, unable to look away. There were shouts and pleas, there was a struggle but Peter could see little of it.

A shot rang out. Peter covered his ears as everyone in the kitchen fell backwards. He sat still for a moment and watched. His mother sat on the floor, leaning against one of the cupboards. Where was his father? And that man?

Hearing muffled voices, Peter thought the shot had made him deaf, then he realised he still had his hands clasped over his ears. He saw his father in the doorway, he was holding something wrapped in a tea towel. Philip marched over to Peter and crouched down in front of him.

"Son, I need you to do something very important," he held the object out towards Peter. "I need you to take this outside and hide it."

Peter realised that it was his mother's pistol. He pulled back and shook his head, refusing to touch it.

"You have to do as I say," his father said firmly. "Your mother could get into a lot of trouble for having this thing." He looked around nervously, as though someone might be watching. "Please," he said, "just take it outside and bury it."

Reluctantly, Peter nodded and grabbed hold of the gun. He stood, but his father stopped him, looking him in the eye.

"When the police come and they ask why you were out there, you tell them that you were hiding, okay? You got scared, and you hid."

Peter nodded and bolted down the hall, through the back door and into the garden.

Philip returned to the kitchen, grabbing the telephone from the counter. Imogen looked up at him as he knelt by her side. She groaned, clutching her stomach, every muscle in her body felt like it was in spasm.

Philip held her close as he dialled 999. He watched as the intruder lay wheezing in a pool of blood. The man tried to lift his head but there was no strength left in him. His eyes continued to stare at Philip as they faded away.

Peter ran to the end of the garden where he dropped to his knees just in front of a tree and began to dig. The rain made it difficult, filling the hole with water and forcing the mud to slide back down to fill it. Eventually, Peter dug deep enough to place the gun and push the remaining mud over to cover it.

The rain was pelting down harder and there was a flash of lightning in the sky followed by a sharp blast of thunder. Peter jumped, the sound of the gunshot still echoing in his mind, but through the downpour he could hear sirens in the distance. Help was on its way.

The lightning flashed again, and with it Peter saw the intruder staring down at him, as clear as he had seen him only moments before. Peter yelped, scrambled to his feet and ran back towards the house. He did not stop to look back at that face, the same face that would haunt him for the next twelve years.

Peter sat on his bed, still pondering what to do. Some time had gone by before he realised that someone else was there with him. He looked up to see his mother, Imogen. She was as he remembered her; tall and elegant with an authoritative air, but a kind face. Peter smiled at her warmly. She smiled back, but folded her arms and raised an eyebrow.

"Why were you keeping hold of that thing?" she asked.

"Protection." Peter replied evenly, but still grinned.

"If 'd known you still had that thing," said Imogen, "there would've been hell to pay."

Peter just shrugged and looked down. Imogen regarded her son for a moment.

"You don't seem all that surprised to see

me," she said.

"To be honest," he replied. "I've kind of been expecting you." He looked up again, meeting her eyes.

"You're beginning to understand, aren't you?" Imogen stepped towards him.

"What's to understand?" Peter stood up and began to pace the room. "I'm beginning to accept it, but I can't understand it." He stopped moving and faced his mother, folding his arms. "I really don't want this."

"Do you think anyone would?" Imogen replied. "Peter, accept the gift that God has given you."

Peter sighed angrily. He never did like talk of gods and demons, and divine powers, the thought of it unsettled him; but his mother believed in it all, so he tried not to show his aggravation.

"I don't think I can deal with this," he said. "I see them all the time, they follow me wherever I go, They even talk to me in my sleep." He threw his arms out in frustration. "They just won't leave me alone!"

Imogen sighed. "It'll be easier when you're ready to listen," she said. Peter sat back down and stared at her blankly. "Just talk to them," she continued. "That's all they want."

Peter rested his head in his hands and let

out a deep breath. “Why me?” he mourned.

“Because you're a good, decent human being,” Imogen replied. “Just make sure you stay that way – don't abuse your gift.”

Peter looked up sharply and shook his head. “I'm astounded that you keep calling it a gift,” he said, coming across much calmer than he actually felt.

“A curse then,” his mother said. “Either way you're here to use it.”

Peter sighed, he did not want to use his so-called gift, or be used by it. However, as he thought about it, it seemed so simple. Talking to Bethany's family at the hospital had been surprisingly easy, as was talking to his own mother now. And the stranger – he had left Peter alone once he had acknowledged him.

“You need to start being honest,” said Imogen.

“And accept who I am,” Peter replied. “I know. I've already had this lecture.”

“That's not what I meant.” Imogen sighed. “You've always bottled up your feelings, what good can that do?”

Peter stared at her, a quizzical expression formed across his face. Imogen continued to regard him intently. “Have you told Bethany how you feel about her?”

“How did you know...?”

“I'm your mother.” Imogen replied.

Peter sighed and slumped his shoulders. It appeared that his feelings were obvious to everyone except Bethany herself. He laughed to himself and shrugged.

“She won't have me.”

“How do you know if you don't ask?” Imogen scoffed. “I didn't bring my son up to be defeatist.”

“She's already made it pretty clear...” Peter protested.

“Has she?” Imogen smiled. Peter looked down, he dreaded the thought of seeing Bethany again, he was afraid to find out for sure. “Just give it some time,” his mother continued. “She has a lot to deal with – and so do you.”

She was right, it had been a rough few weeks for everyone. Peter wondered if things would ever seem normal again. His thoughts went back over the last weeks and he reminded himself of the gun. He needed to deal with that first.

“You need to get that gun back.” Imogen prodded, as though reading his mind.

“You think I don't know that?” Peter said irritably.

“I think you know where to find it,” she said. “We can fix this.”

"We?" Peter replied, finally looking up from the floor. He shook his head. "This is my mess," he said. "I should fix it."

"You wouldn't be in this mess if it wasn't for me."

"Don't," he said. "That's not fair."

"I'll tell you what's not fair," Imogen spat. "Your father doing time for protecting his family."

Peter could feel the rage radiating from her. Even after so many years it still made them both angry. The law had come down on Philip Crossgrave because he chose to help his wife while the man who broke into their home bled to death. He had grabbed the gun and it had fired; it was never clear who squeezed the trigger. The judge saw fit to give him the harshest sentence possible. He had protected his family at the cost of his own freedom, something which Imogen constantly, and remorsefully, thought about. "I only hope that I did my best for you," she said after a time.

"You did," Peter replied, his voice barely louder than a whisper.

"Then at least it wasn't for nothing," she said.

They looked at each other and remained silent for a while, they both knew what was about to come.

"I have to go now," Imogen said.

"I know." Peter replied.

"Next time you see your father send him my love."

"I will." Peter smiled broadly, he wondered how his father would react to that message. Peter said his final goodbyes to his mother, then she was gone.

He sat and contemplated everything that had happened. His mother was right, he had a very good idea of where he could find that gun. Once he found it he would just have the problem of disposing of it. He cursed himself, wishing he had left it buried in the garden all those years ago.

Kevin walked along the promenade on The Watch, Karen was sat on the wall opposite the statue of Gabriel, waiting for him. As she saw him approach, Karen slid down from the wall, ran over to Kevin and threw her arms around him. Her hugged her back.

"Did you find it?" she asked, looking up at him hopefully.

"Yeah," he nodded. "It was right where you said it would be."

"Good." Karen looked up at him and

smiled.

Kevin cupped her face in his hands and kissed her forehead. He sighed heavily. “Do you think that what we're doing is wrong?”

Karen pulled back. “How can you say that?” she said defensively. “How can it be wrong when we love each other?”

“It's just all this secrecy,” Kevin sighed. “Why do we have to hide it? I hate it.”

Karen furrowed her brow. “You haven't told anyone, have you?”

“No,” said Kevin. “Of course I haven't!”

“Good.” Karen circled her arms around Kevin's waist and laid her head on his chest. “It'll all be over soon.”

“Soon,” Kevin agreed, returning her embrace and stroking her hair. “I promise.”

Karen looked up at him expectantly. “The sooner the better, I think.”

“There are a few things I have to sort out first,” Kevin said, trying to sound reassuring he added: “Tonight.”

Karen smiled and nodded. She looked up into Kevin's eyes and kissed him, he held onto her, both content with the knowledge that everything would soon be put right.

Bethany smiled as Peter walked into the

room, but her face dropped as he nodded vaguely in her direction. he seemed agitated.

"I brought your things," he said, dropping a bag onto the end of the bed.

"Pete, what's up?" Bethany asked.

Peter paced agitatedly for a few moments before stopping to grab hold of the bars at the foot of the bed. He glared at Bethany, and looking around to make sure no one was within earshot, Peter lowered his voice. "The gun's gone."

"What?" Bethany leaned forward. "What do you mean it's gone? I thought you got rid of it?"

"I was going to get rid of it, but it's gone." Peter stared at her accusingly. "Have you moved it?"

"I haven't touched the thing, I wouldn't!" she folded her arms in disgust and, forgetting that the left one was in a cast, winced as she tried to ignore the pain that was now shooting up her arm. "I thought you got rid of it," she repeated.

"Did you tell anyone?"

Bethany looked away but she could tell he was still staring at her, she got the impression that there was more to this attack than he was letting on.

"Of course I didn't tell anyone." She huffed

and glared back at Peter. “Perhaps you told someone?”

“No.” He shook his head. “Not me.

“Well, neither did I!” Bethany protested. “Pete, I didn't tell anyone, you know I didn't.”

Peter looked at her and shrugged. He knew that she was telling the truth, he did not know why he felt the sudden urge to accuse her. He had let his anger lay dormant all day, spending the morning worrying about her and the afternoon divided between admiring and cursing her. Peter was unsure how he would feel when he first saw her, but he had allowed all his negative emotions to rise to the surface when he walked in and saw her smile – like nothing had happened.

Realising that he was still gripping the bed frame, Peter let go and began to pace again. Bethany sighed as she watched her friend.

“Pete, what's gotten into you?”

He stopped and stared, almost looking through her. “I have to go,” he said flatly. “I know who to ask about it.”

As Peter made to leave, Bethany sighed. She knew him better than that. “Pete!” she called. “Are you going to tell me what's really wrong?”

Peter stood by the door, his hand rested on the jamb, his shoulders hunched as he clenched his fist by his side. Should he tell her why he was angry? Perhaps it was better left unsaid.

"Peter?" Bethany prodded.

He sighed heavily and without turning to look at her, he said: "You broke my heart when you left this morning."

Bethany's heart knotted. She had not realised that he felt that way, but as she heard him say the words it all made sense. She thought back to all the times when he had offered her support when she needed it. He was there, every time – even when she did not want him to be. He was calm and sensitive, and sometimes even overprotective. Of course he loved her. How could she not know?

She had done things to hurt herself, which was bad enough, but now she had hurt her closest friend too. She wanted to tell him she was sorry, but that somehow did not seem to be enough. Either way, he would not give her that chance. Without looking back, he walked away. Bethany called after him, but it went unanswered, she was left to sit alone once more. She had woken up this morning thinking she had made a stupid mistake; she now realised that it was the biggest mistake she had ever made.

* * *

Peter pushed through the gate at the Marshall residence. He was still seething, though he regretted the way he had handled the situation with Bethany. He hoped that he could deal with the next one better. He knew he had to focus on the matter at hand, he knew exactly who to ask about the missing gun. Peter was about to knock on the door when he heard a soft voice behind him.

"Don't," it warned.

Peter turned to see a girl of about sixteen. She was fair-haired and pale skinned, and looked eerily familiar. It took him a few seconds to realise who she was. The girl smiled.

"You do recognise me, don't you, Peter?"

He nodded. "Karen Marshall."

"Don't get involved," she said. Her smile became cocky, sneering, as she stepped towards him. "Just leave it alone."

"You know I can't do that."

"There's nothing you can do," said Karen. "Kevin and I are going to be together, so just walk away – forget you ever knew anything."

Peter regarded her disdainfully. Bethany had been right, Kevin's behaviour had been unusual lately and Peter guessed that Karen was more than likely to be the cause of it. He scowled at her. "It was you who told him where to find the gun, wasn't it?"

"And you told me," she replied, a smug grin creeping across her face. "People are so impressionable in their sleep."

Peter ignored her taunts, seeing it as a tactic for diversion, and banged loudly on the door. When there was no answer, he knocked again.

Karen began to laugh. "There is nothing you can do to keep us from being together."

Peter refused to acknowledge the girl and continued to pound on the door until it was thrown open by an angry-looking Amanda Marshall.

"What do you think you're playing at?!" she yelled over the screaming infant in her arms. "I'm trying to get Maisie to sleep!"

"I'm sorry, Mrs. Marshall," Peter replied, "but it's very important that I speak to Kevin."

"Well, if he didn't answer the bloody door, he's clearly not home!"

Peter stopped the door with his hand as Amanda tried to close it. Pushing past her, he rushed through the hall and up the stairs. Amanda furiously slammed the door and followed him.

As he reached the top landing, Peter paused. Karen stood in front of Kevin's bedroom door, a grotesque smile twisted her face.

"Nothing you can do will keep us from being together."

Karen vanished as Peter lunged forward. He pushed the door open and dashed into Kevin's room. He was not there. Amanda rushed into the room a second later.

"Peter Crossgrave! You can't just walk in here and-" she stopped and stared, clutched Maisie close to her chest. The child's wailing had quickly subsided into a mere grizzle, then stopped altogether.

"Oh, my God," Amanda whispered. She and Peter stood side by side and gazed silently around the room. Hundreds of pictures were pinned to the wall. There was a small cluster of old photographs in the centre of one wall. Spread out across the rest of the room were drawings; angels. Correction; myriad images of one angel. Peter stepped forward to inspect some of the pictures more closely. The photographs he ignored, but the sketches he looked at further. The subject was older than in the photographs, but it was unmistakeable. Karen.

"What is this?" Slowly shaking her head,

Amanda stared dumbly at the images in front of her.

"I think it's a cry for help." Peter knew that his friend was planning to do something stupid, but when? Where had he gone? For a moment Peter had the sickening feeling that he was too late, but he realised he had time. Karen was still there. As long as she attempted to scupper his progress, Peter knew that there was hope of finding Kevin alive.

Karen stood next to Peter, smiling and gazing at her portraits. "Isn't my brother talented?"

He ignored her, focusing on the sketches. If he was right, if this was a cry for help, then there must be some clue pointing to where Kevin might be. Peter was sure his friend would have left some kind of message and he was determined to find it.

Karen let out a short, self-satisfied laugh. She raised herself up on tip-toes and whispered in Peter's ear. "Nothing you can do will keep us from being together."

Peter sneered and stepped away from her, studying the pictures in front of him. Then he saw it. One of the angels looked different from the others. This was not a portrait of Karen; It was Gabriel.

He turned to face Amanda; she was

shivering, angry, frightened. Tears welled up in her eyes and she breathed deeply, fighting them back, desperate not to cry in front of her son's friend.

"I think I know where he is."

"So what?" Karen sounded bored. "There's nothing you can do..."

Amanda seemed not to have heard him.

"Mrs. Marshall?" Peter place his hand on her shoulder. She turned her head and stared at him blankly. She was in shock. Peter knew there was no time to talk her round, he had to act now.

"I'll find him and bring him home," he said. Turning to Karen, he added: "That's a promise."

She sneered and arched an eyebrow. He would fail, she was sure of it. The Watch was a big place, Kevin was up there somewhere and Peter had to reach him before Karen. That was an almost impossible task.

Without another word to Amanda, Peter rushed from the bedroom. Even as he pelted down the stairs he could still hear Karen's voice.

"NOTHING YOU CAN DO WILL KEEP US FROM BEING TOGETHER!"

17.
Moving On

1992

Kevin sat in his room with the door shut. Karen was with him, she shifted nervously from where she sat on the floor.

"Is this going to hurt?" she asked as Kevin took out his pocket knife.

"You might feel a little prick," said Kevin, "but I promise it'll only hurt for a second."

"What'll we tell mum?"

"Nothing." Kevin shrugged. "If she notices, just tell her you fell or something."

Karen shuffled, still feeling uneasy, Kevin tried to reassure her. "It's okay," he said. "I'll go first so you can see that it doesn't hurt."

Karen nodded silently as she watched Kevin flick open the blade of his pocket knife. He poked the tip into the palm of his left hand and a tiny bead of blood formed around it. After a fraction of a second, the pain kicked in. The sharp, burning sensation faded into a dull throb just as soon as it had started.

"Ow!" Kevin flinched and shook his hand

as though trying to expel the pain from his body. He stopped after a second and turned to his sister.

"You see?" he said. "That didn't hurt."

Karen raised her eyebrows and said nothing. Her brother had not filled her with confidence. Kevin reached out his hand. "Come on," he said, "your turn."

Karen sat back with her arms tightly folded and she shook her head firmly.

"I won't hurt you, I promise," he said. Reluctantly, she gave Kevin her hand and squeezed her eyes shut. Karen felt the tip of the knife dig into her palm and she immediately pulled away.

"Ow!" She held one hand in the other and stared at the tiny drop of blood that pooled in her palm. Karen shook herself out of her daze and she realised that Kevin was trying to get her attention.

"Hello?!" he said, holding his palm up and waving it in front of her. "Together forever?"

Karen lifted her hand to her brother's and their fingers intertwined. "Together forever." she repeated.

"We'll never be apart," said Kevin.

* * *

Peter raced up the steep slopes of The Watch in a frantic search for his friend. He was out of breath by the time he reached the top, but he had to keep going. The promenade was deserted, that left the church yard. Peter was glad to see that his instincts had been right, he found Kevin at the back of the church, sitting cross-legged on the ground. He stared at the gun he held in his hands. Peter approached him cautiously.

"Kevin?"

His friend looked up at him, his eyes seemed glazed over, like he was already somewhere else.

"Kevin, what are you doing?" He stepped a little closer. Kevin appeared to be in such a stupor that Peter thought he could easily take the gun from his hands. He just needed to get close enough first.

"I'm moving on," Kevin said absently. "It's better this way."

Peter had known what Kevin intended to do before he found him, but now that he faced the situation he felt sick, lost. He had to do everything in his power to stop his friend from doing this, but he did not know where to begin.

"I can't let you do this," was all he could think of to say. He took another step forward and Kevin stood up and backed away.

"Don't." He shook his head fiercely. Peter stayed still and watched him for a moment, unsure of what to do next.

"I can't let her go," Kevin said at last, "not again. This is the only way."

"No, it's not," said Peter. "She's not coming back and nothing you can do can change that. You have to let her go."

"Don't listen to him." Karen emerged from the trees and stood between the two of them. Peter wondered how long she had been there before showing herself. She glanced disdainfully at Peter before moving to stand by Kevin's side.

"He doesn't want us to be happy," she cooed.

Kevin began to twitch, he smiled nervously. "Why don't you want us to be happy, Pete?"

"What are you talking about?" Peter frowned, he desperately needed to reach his friend. How? What if anything Peter said made things worse?

Karen stood by her brother and smiled at Peter as though she had beaten him to a coveted prize. He could not let her manipulate his friend like this. He had to think of something.

With Bethany it had been simple, she understood what was happening to her, but Kevin... Peter could not convince him that Karen was out for her own gain, no matter what the consequences for anyone else. She held too much power over him.

"I need to be with her," Kevin said.

Peter felt his stomach knot inside him. His friend was already lost and there was nothing he could do to stop it.

"What's this going to achieve?" he said, his tone desperate, defeated.

"We'll both be happy," Kevin replied.

"You'll both be dead," Peter blurted out without thinking. He did not regret it though, he had his friend's attention. Kevin's eyes seemed to focus for the first time since Peter found him.

"She's not really gone." He smiled crookedly, cast Karen a glance. "I'm not mad," he added, "she's right here." Kevin's arm shook as he gripped the gun tightly, turning his knuckles white. He waved in Karen's direction. "Tell me you can see her!"

"Go on, Peter," Karen smirked. "Tell him."

Ignoring the infuriating girl, Peter regarded his friend for a moment. Kevin's eyes silently pleaded with him, he wanted Peter to tell him that he had not gone insane. In a sense, he had; Karen had driven him that way.

What could he do? Peter needed to drive a wedge between the siblings, weaken their bond, destroy Karen's hold over her brother. But how? He could not compete with her persuasive skills. She must have been working on Kevin for years, whispering in his ear, reinforcing his guilt, sending him mad.

That was it.

Insanity could be temporary. He had to convince Kevin that he needed help, that there was another way out of his misery. Peter sighed and looked through Karen, shaking his head slightly.

"Marshall, there's no one there."

"He's lying!" Karen moved to stand in front Kevin, forcing him to focus his attention on her. "He doesn't want us to be together."

Kevin stared blankly into Karen's eyes, she looked into his, pleading with him.

"Are you listening to me?" said Peter.

Kevin looked up, throwing his arms out as though presenting Karen to him. "But she's right there..." He broke away from her and began to pace back and forth.

"It'll all be over soon," Karen said in a comforting tone which Peter found horrifying.

"Kevin!" he yelled, bringing his friend to a halt. Kevin's eyes seemed to go out of focus, he stared past Peter, frowning and shaking his head. He began to play with the gun, absently twirling it around with his finger through the trigger guard. Peter took a sharp breath as he imagined Kevin shooting himself through the foot.

"Why don't you give me the gun?" Peter held out his hand in the vain hope that Kevin would relinquish the weapon.

"Don't give it to him." Karen moved to stand behind Kevin and whispered to him. "He'll do anything to try to stop us." She glared at Peter, who chose to ignore her. Kevin stopped fiddling with the gun, looked down at the ground and shook his head violently. Either Karen was there and he had to make things right, or she was not and he had lost his mind. He was unsure which one was worse.

"I know you miss your sister..." Peter moved forward slowly.

"No! You don't understand!" Kevin yelled, waving the gun carelessly. Peter took a step back, Kevin sighed and let his arm drop to his side. "I've failed her."

"No, you haven't." Peter replied. "There's

nothing that you could have done."

Kevin perched on a tombstone and stared down at his feet. Peter wondered if he had heard a word he had just said.

"She's here," Kevin said weakly. It seemed as though she had always been there. Kevin could imagine how she would be, from the way she looked right down to her scent. She knew things that only Karen could know. She was not just in his head, she was real.

"Marshall..." Peter's weary tone snapped Kevin out of his trance.

"Don't tell me it's all in my head, Pete," Kevin protested. "She's here."

"That's right." Karen simpered. "I'm here."

"Tell me I'm crazy, Pete."

"Okay, you're crazy." The second he uttered that sentence, Peter realised that was probably not a smart move. He may have just undone any progress he had made with him.

Karen pouted and moved to stand next to Kevin, he shuddered as she took hold of his arm.

"Don't listen to him," she whispered as she glared at Peter.

"Kevin, I'm sorry," he said desperately. "You have to listen to me. You have to let it go. Move on"

"I can't." Kevin shook his head. "I need to

make things right."

"Make what right?!" Peter asked despairingly. "You haven't done anything wrong."

Kevin sighed, stood up and began to pace again. "When she died," he said, "a part of me died too."

"It's natural to feel that way..."

"Don't pretend to know how I feel!" Kevin shouted, waving the gun again. Peter took a step back and began to feel his anger seeping to the surface once more, and once again, it would be directed at someone who did not deserve it.

"Of course I know how you feel!" he yelled back at him. "You're not the only one who's lost someone!" Peter managed to stop himself from saying any more, but furious thoughts still stampeded through his mind. He had lost his family too and on top of that, Peter had to watch his friends fall apart. Bethany had lost everything that mattered to her and Kevin had experienced a similar fate; except he still had someone left, and if he did what he intended to do, that someone would be devastated.

Kevin shook his head. "You don't understand."

"Of course he doesn't," Karen told him.

"I'm the only one who understands you."

"Karen understands..."

"Karen is gone!" Peter yelled, desperately trying to hammer the point into Kevin's head.

"I'm still here!" Karen snapped venomously. "I'm right here and you know it!"

Karen glared at Peter as he did his best to ignore her while Kevin looked back and forth between the two. Regardless of whether Karen was really there or not, Kevin could not go on like this. His guilt and sadness had kept her spirit alive, whether he was crazy, whether she was real did not matter any more. Taking a deep breath, trying to fight back the tears that he had bottled up inside himself for so many years, Kevin put the gun to his head.

Peter took a step forward, but did not know what he could do that would not result in someone being injured – or worse.

"I'm sorry, Pete," Kevin said, shaking his head remorsefully. "I can't do this any more."

"That's it," Karen came to stand behind him once more to whisper her poison in his ear. "It'll be quick and painless, and then it'll all be over. You and me can be together."

Peter took another step forward. "Kevin, don't do this."

Kevin stepped away, not saying anything, only shaking his head. He hesitated. Kevin's whole body shook, Peter could tell that he was not going to pull the trigger, he could see it in his eyes. Kevin was terrified, he would not take his own life – unless he was pushed.

"Pull the trigger," Karen said softly.

"Kevin, don't do this you selfish bastard!"

Kevin snapped out of his trance and lowered the gun, finally giving Peter his full attention. Karen let out a noise that was somewhere between a scream and a growl.

"I mean it," said Peter. "Have you thought about your mum? She's already lost one child, do you think she needs to lose you too?"

"Don't." Kevin spoke through gritted teeth. Peter was relieved to see that the gun remained at his side - for now.

"Your mum needs you, Kevin."

"Forget her!" Karen spat, "I'm your sister! I need you!"

Kevin was lost, he had no idea which way to turn. He had known and trusted Peter throughout most of his life, but then there was Karen.

"I told her I'd always be there to look after her," he said.

"You were," Peter replied. "You did your

best for her, but she's not here any more."

"He's lying!" Karen was becoming more desperate and hysterical by the minute. "He doesn't want us to be together, but if you pull that trigger we will be." Kevin did not look at her but continued to stare at Peter, Karen's tone became a high-pitched whining. "I'm your sister. Please..."

"Kevin, this is the coward's way out," said Peter. "Don't do this."

"I don't want to do this," he replied, "but I don't know what else to do."

"Pull the trigger!" Karen became enraged and stepping in front of Kevin, she raised her right hand, showing him the scar that was embedded in her palm. "You made me a promise, Kevin!"

"You can keep going," Peter said. "That's all you can do."

Kevin crouched to the floor and broke down. His held his head in his free hand. "I miss her," he wailed.

"I know," Peter replied. "Just let her go."

"I miss you too," Karen whined. "That's why you have to come with me."

"She should be here, Pete." Kevin said, eventually looking up. "Karen always did everything that I did, and I encouraged her. Mum said she was like my shadow, she followed me everywhere. If it wasn't for me..."

Peter sighed and crouched down opposite his friend, making sure to position himself between brother and sister. "You know it wasn't your fault."

"I should have been looking out for her..."

"You were," Peter protested. "There is nothing that you could have done to prevent it. I was there, remember? It was an accident, that's all."

Kevin knew that, but he could not help thinking about it, playing it over and over in his mind. He slumped with his back against a headstone and stared at the gun for a while. He released his grip on the butt and held it lightly in both hands.

"Don't you dare give him that gun!" Karen screeched. Kevin handed the weapon to Peter who grabbed it and shoved it into his belt at the small of his back before Kevin changed his mind.

"But... but, I'm your sister..." Karen huffed sulkily and stamped her foot. Peter moved to sit next to Kevin and sat there silently until his friend was ready to speak.

Kevin felt as though he were waking up from living nightmare. His family life had been a shambles the last eight years; his sister had died, his father had left and just as he and his mother were getting used to being on their own, his father came back. The next few years were strained at best, and after the baby was born, Kevin Marshall senior vanished for the second time and they did not hear from him again.

"My family's falling apart," Kevin said at last.

"And how is offing yourself going to help?" Peter replied flatly. Kevin turned his head to look at him and managed a tiny, nervous smile. He felt ashamed, and so he should.

"What would your mum do if she lost another child?" Peter continued, "don't do that to her."

Kevin sighed. Peter was right, his mother had suffered enough with the loss of a child and a husband who had left her twice. She could only cope now because Kevin had been there to help her out.

"I know," he said at last. "I'm being selfish."

"I know it hasn't been easy," said Peter. "Just talk to your mum."

Kevin let out a long weary sigh. "I don't know what to say to her." He said after a while.

"You'll think of something," Peter reassured him. Silence descended upon them again and after a while, Peter came to realise that Karen was nowhere to be seen. "Kev, you don't see your sister now, do you?"

Kevin laughed. "Dude, I'm not that fucking crazy!"

"Just checking." Peter grinned and slapped his friend on the shoulder. "Come on, I promised your mum I'd get you home in one piece."

Bethany lay on the bed, staring at the wall opposite, alone with her own thoughts. She was waiting to be discharged from the hospital, but she was not quite ready to leave yet. She felt lousy, but for different reasons than before, she was unsure of what to do with herself.

She rolled over and lay back on the bed, staring up at the ceiling, counting the tiles for the umpteenth time. Ninety-six and a half, or thereabouts. She had been waiting there a long time, perhaps the nurses had forgotten about her, not that Bethany cared, she wanted to be left alone for as long as possible. She shut her eyes and let her mind wander, but eventually, Bethany's train of thought was interrupted by one of the nurses.

"Bethany?" He shook her gently, "are you awake?"

"Yeah," she sat up. "I'm awake."

"You'll be please to know you're free to go."

"Great." Bethany returned his smile, though somewhat unenthusiastically.

As the nurse left, Bethany sighed and began to gather her belongings. Sitting in the chair next to the bed, she pulled on her Dr. Marten boots. It was difficult one handed, the boots were on her feet but she struggled with the laces. She would have to ask one of the nurses for help or she would never be ready to go.

Go where? Bethany was certain that she was no longer welcome at Peter's house and she had no intention of going back to Brian. She was in danger of feeling sorry for herself when she heard a familiar voice.

"Hey, ready to go?"

Bethany looked up and was surprised to see Peter standing in the doorway.

"You came back?" she said.

"Of course I came back." Peter laughed. "You didn't think I was going to leave you to make your own way home, did you?"

Bethany shrugged. She wanted to run over

to Peter and hug him, but she thought better of it, so she sat there and looked down at her feet.

Without a word, Peter knelt down and finished tying her laces. She watched him silently; how grateful she was that he was still there.

Peter looked up at her. “You look better.”

Bethany looked healthier than she had done for weeks. Peter could not help but look her over as she sat there in her combats and hooded sweater, and her faded hair with many different colours. She would say she looked a mess but to Peter, this was Bethany at her beautiful best. He had to forget about that for now, though, he knew that there were other things on her mind.

Bethany did feel better in many ways, but she still felt a number of things biting at the back of her mind. She grew impatient with the pleasantries, that was not their style.

“I'm sorry, Pete,” she said quickly, “I didn't know...”

Peter sighed and stood, taking hold of Bethany's hand and helping her to her feet.

“I'll live.”

Bethany knew that he was more hurt than he was letting on. She was hurting too, although she never meant to cause Peter any pain because of it. She had only wanted comfort and had gone the wrong way about getting it.

"I really need you as my friend, Peter," she said. "I don't want anything to change that."

Of course Peter understood that, Bethany did not need any more complications in her life. Realising that, however, did not ease his pain. He chose not to show it, he was sure it would pass with time.

"I know," was all he said.

"I really didn't think you'd come back," said Bethany.

"We're still friends," Peter replied. "Always."

"I couldn't go back to live with Brian again," she continued. "I couldn't face going back there..." Bethany breathed deep in an attempt to fight back the tears that began to well up. Peter took her in his arms, the first real contact between them since the night before.

"I'd never let you go back there," he said. "You know that."

Bethany held him tighter and began to sob. "Oh, God! Why, Pete?" she wailed. "Why did he do it?!"

"It's okay, I'm here." Peter could think of nothing to say to console her, he could only hold her close. Anything that had happened between them seemed insignificant; seeing her like this was what truly broke his heart.

"What did I do?" she cried. "What did I do to make him do that to me?"

"It wasn't your fault, Beth," Peter said. "You did nothing to deserve that. No one deserves that."

"I keep thinking," she said, after pausing for a few breaths, "that if I had behaved better or something..."

"Don't even think that." Peter felt sick at the thought of all the things Brian had done to her, even now she was affected by it. Peter had thought that it would all be over as soon as Bethany was away from her uncle, but he now realised it would take more than that to help her heal.

"What if I end up like him?" Bethany said quietly.

Peter frowned, how could she let these thoughts cross her mind? "How can you even compare yourself to him?" he asked

"Oh, come on." Bethany looked up at him. "What's the first thing I do when I have a problem? I go out and get off my face so I can try to forget about it. You'd think I'd have learned by now that it doesn't work." She sighed and looked down. "I'm going to end up just as pathetic as he is."

"Don't say that," Peter replied. "Brian's just a crazy old drunk who doesn't know how to deal with his own problems. You're nothing like him."

Bethany shrugged.

"Come on," said Peter. "You know you'll never be like him. You're too good, and sweet, and kind..." He wondered if she was listening to him, he cupped Bethany's face in his hands, making her look him in the eye. "Beth, you are so strong, I know you can get through this."

Sighing heavily, Bethany let some silent tears flow, she had cried so many times in front of Peter these last few weeks that she saw no reason to hold them back. Her friends had always thought of her as strong, but through all the fighting and surviving she felt so weak and tired.

Circling her good arm around Peter's waist, Bethany rested her head on his chest and let out a weary sigh. "I'm broken."

Peter wrapped his arms around her. "And we'll fix you."

"I just want it to go away," she whispered.

"I know," he replied. "It just takes time."

"I hope you're right." The way she felt at that moment, Bethany could see no end, she just had to keep walking in the right direction – wherever that was. Peter said nothing and held her tight, but before too long, they pulled apart.

"Ready to go?" he asked. Bethany smiled and nodded, he kissed her on the forehead.

"Okay," he said. "Let's get the hell out of here."

Peter and Bethany walked arm in arm along the corridor. To Peter the air felt cold and he knew why. Hospitals were full of the newly departed but he did not want to see them, not today. He kept his head down as they made as quickly as they could towards the exit.

Once outside, Peter hailed a taxi. He opened the door for Bethany and helped her slide into the back seat. Before getting into the cab himself, Peter noticed someone standing across the road, staring at him. It was Karen.

Not the same sixteen year old that had just yesterday attempted to coerce his close friend into suicide, but Karen as he remembered her when they were children. She glared at Peter. Still the same girl, sweetness and light just so long as she had her own way. She faded from view and Peter smiled to himself. If he ever saw her again it would be too soon. He got into the waiting taxi and he and Bethany headed home.

Kevin stood and stared at the pictures on his bedroom wall. When and how he had become so obsessed he did not know. He had spoken to his mother on a level that he never had before and that had made things easier. Distancing himself from those who cared for him had only made him crazy.

His family had been torn apart, but he could have made things much worse. Kevin began to realise that his love for his sister and desire to be with her were obsessive and unhealthy. His will to live was still at a low ebb, but there was also the tiniest will to survive, and that was enough.

One by one, he began to tear the pictures down from the wall. He stopped when he reached a particular photograph – one of Karen, himself, Peter and Bethany, taken when they were children – not long before Karen died. This was the only picture of his sister that Kevin kept.

Peter walked along the side of the canal. He found a quiet spot and making sure there was no one around, he reached into his jacket pocket. He pulled out the gun that he had wrapped in a plastic bag to conceal it.

Looking around once more to make certain that he was alone, Peter flung the wretched weapon into the water. He thought of how differently things could have turned out as he watched the gun sink to the bottom of the canal.

Sean packed a bag for himself and Jack. He felt he could no longer stay in this town with the guilt of Nicole hanging over his head. He had felt her presence since he had moved there, but since his confrontation with Peter, that presence now felt stronger.

He was not sure where he was going to go or what he was going to do. All he knew was that he needed to take his son somewhere where no one knew who they were. So Sean took Jack, a small bag and the clothes on their backs, and shut the door to their old life.

A man walked his dog through the wooded area of the church yard on The Watch. The small springer spaniel disappeared into the bushes and started to bark. The owner called out to his dog, but he stayed put and continued to howl.

The man eventually had to make his way through the undergrowth to retrieve his dog. Pushing through the bushes, he saw the body of a young, blonde woman.

Natalie lay under the willow tree where she and Alex often sat. Her skin was cold and turning blue, and her muscles were beginning to stiffen. An empty pill bottle lay next to her lifeless body.

Brian leaned against the door jamb and stared vacantly into Bethany's empty room. Many days had passed before he had even realised that she had gone, and he did not know where to.

He muttered to himself and made for the front room, where he opened a half-finished bottle of vodka. He sat down on the sofa, turned on the television and started to drink.

Bethany sat in the back of the cab with Peter sitting silently next to her. Both looked out of opposite windows as the taxi drove them away from the hospital.

The Watch slowly appeared along the

horizon and Bethany caught a glimpse of the angel statue through the trees. The stone statue of the Archangel Gabriel could be clearly seen from the town. The Watch, where she stood was the highest point for miles around. She was the angel of mercy and retribution and a guide to those who have lost their way. Bethany felt that she could do with a guide like that in her life.

As the car drove along the foot of The Watch, she looked over at Peter, who was still staring out of the window. His hand rested lightly on the seat next to him, Bethany reached out for it. As her fingers encircled his, Peter stared at Bethany who looked back at him with hopeful eyes. She squeezed his hand, he squeezed back. Neither of them said a word, they did not have to.

The last few weeks had been a trying time for everyone, and although they knew that nothing would ever be the same again, they felt sure that everything would work out for the best. It was just going to take some time.

About the author

Sandra Dee Sims was born in Aberdeen, Scotland and now lives in Hertfordshire, England. She has a degree in Media Technology and worked in television and radio for several years before setting up a small jewellery business.

When she's not writing or making jewellery, Sandra enjoys gaming, kayaking, playing the ukulele, and geeking over Star Trek.

COMING SOON

ANGEL WALK

A schoolgirl is missing without a trace.

A small woods lies along part of Angel Walk, an idyllic coastal path. Here, a body has been found and it is feared that this may be the missing teenager.

Peter already knows. He has a gift that only he and his closest friends know about.

Bethany thought her troubles were over. Some unexpected news drags up memories she would rather forget.

Esme tries to carry on as normal. The loss of her sister has affected her in more ways than she can explain.

As the events surrounding the missing girl unfold, the three of them find themselves involved and it soon becomes clear that the situation is more sinister than any of them could have imagined. Can they find a way to help and if so, will there be a price to pay?

www.ingramcontent.com/pod-product-compliance
Ingram Content Group UK Ltd.
Pitfield, Milton Keynes, MK11 3LW, UK
UKHW020223250726
13967UKWH00001B/149

9 780993 050008